Druids Hill

Druids Hill

Carl Tighe

Five Leaves Crime

www.fiveleaves.co.uk

Druids Hill
by Carl Tighe

Published in 2008 by
Five Leaves Publications,
PO Box 8786, Nottingham NG1 9AW
www.fiveleaves.co.uk

ISBN: 978 1 905512 55 3

Five Leaves acknowledges financial support
from Arts Council England

Five Leaves is a member of Inpress
(www.inpressbooks.co.uk),
representing independent publishers.

Design and typeset by Four Sheets
Printed in Great Britain

Many years ago...

Wayne Somerfield was a cheerful fourteen-year old. Like most kids of his age his head was filled with stuff: gadgets and statistics, mostly. Girls he had noticed, but they interested him only in a vague sort of way. They did not understand things, they were not interested in stuff and that was really all he had registered about them. No, girls had not quite hit home yet. But he had been given a brand new BMX bike for Christmas — an 'off road' special with fat tyres, front wheel suspension and more gears than he knew what to do with, and that made him absolutely purr with happiness.

He had recently come to understand that there were other things he wanted, things he could not rely on Christmas and birthdays to get for him. If he wanted socks and sweaters and an encyclopaedia then that would probably be what Christmas and birthdays would bring, and that was OK. But for real stuff, well, for real stuff you had to have another system. His parents had done well with the bike, it was true, but the number of times he had had to make sure of the colour, the saddle, the gears, the make, even.... No, he could not do that every time. He just knew he could not rely on anyone else to choose exactly the right thing. And the stuff he wanted cost money. Real money. He had to be able to buy things — the things he really wanted, the important things — for himself.

So as soon as he was old enough he had got himself a paper round. And now he was saving up, just as hard as he could, for a walkman. Mainly this meant that he had stopped buying sweets on his way home from school. He had also cancelled his subscription to various comics. He still liked comics, but somehow they did not hold his attention in the way they once had. His mother did not want him to do the paper round. She said it might be dangerous, she said you never knew what might happen, and in the winter on that bike he might slip and so early in the morning he might be lying there injured and who would know and he might freeze to death. But his dad said it was OK, he was growing up and anyway by the time he had saved enough to buy a walkman they would be out of fashion and it would be something else. But he had to promise his mother he would be careful and he would watch the road and all that sort of thing. And his dad said:

"And if you come off the bike and you get your leg all scraped don't come home skriking, OK? Or your mother'll want the bike taking off yer."

The fact was he loved being out so early. He loved being up and awake and out and about before anyone else. He said hello to the milkman and most mornings that would be the only person he met. His bag was heavy, the paper-round covered a wide area, without the bike it would not be possible, but at Christmas he had picked up lots of tips, so he was happy.

Panting, Wayne cycled slowly and painfully up the steep slope towards the house at the top of Druids Hill. Never mind, he thought, I can freewheel all the way home. This was his last delivery. He had several papers for the house: *The Guardian* and the mysteriously pink *Financial Times*. There were also a couple of foreign papers. Wayne had looked at them at first, wondering what language they were in. Not French. He did French at school, and he thought he would recognise it even if he could not understand much. Spanish, or maybe Italian, he thought. But he had stopped wondering about them. Now he did not think of them at all. They were just more papers in his bag, waiting for delivery.

He cycled past the standing stone circle, which gleamed eerily in the early morning light. His class had come up here once as part of a history lesson. One day, he thought, one day I will see the ghosts of old Druids dancing round the stones, chanting, their beards flapping, their robes flowing and they'll be preparing for a blood sacrifice and the victim will be lying drugged with mistletoe on the altar and maybe there will be a Roman centurian and he'll come charging in on the Druids, waving his sword. Wayne reached the start of the gravelled driveway. He dismounted, leaned his bike against the ornate stone pillar and noticed rather vaguely that the huge wrought iron gates were shut. Usually they were left open.

He could have driven his bike up the drive, but he preferred to walk. Cycling on gravel was very hard work, with a zillion or even a gazillion gears. He had tried it, and found that in low gear he had to peddle very fast, but peddling very fast while carrying a newspaper bag meant he wobbled, and when he wobbled on gravel he fell off. He didn't do himself any damage, no-one had seen. But his dignity was offended. So now he preferred to walk. He was sure that at this time of the morning his bike, left unlocked at the bottom of the drive, would be safe.

As he crunched up the drive, past the towering trees and spooky bushes, he registered that his feet inside his Wellingtons were very cold and clammy. His mother had warned him to put on two pairs of socks, but he had ignored her. Ah well, never mind, he thought, last delivery, and then soon I'll be home and warm tucking into cereal and hot milk. As he reached the top of the drive he noticed a van parked at the side of the house. He had never seen any vehicle of any kind at Druids Hill. In his imagination he could only ever think of a coach and horses pulling up outside this vast mansion. A van seemed out of place.

He began pulling newspapers out of his bag and folding them ready to push through the letter box, but as he reached the enormous front door with its huge iron knocker and its stained glasses, he noticed what looked like blood on the front step. He crunched glass under foot and, looking up, saw that several of the stained glasses in the front door were missing. Good sense told him that he should drop the papers, get on his bike, get away from there, go home or call the cops from a phone box. The thought flashed through his mind: where is the nearest phone box? Miles away, came the answer. And what if

7

someone is bleeding? Maybe bleeding to death. There's broken glass and blood. It's possible.

And as he was thinking this he registered a smell. He could not place it at first. Something burning? Something burnt? What was that smell? It was sort of familiar, almost but not quite a smell he knew. It was the smell of bacon. Burnt bacon. Had somebody burnt their breakfast? If they had it was no business of his. He pushed the papers through the letter box and turned to go. But suddenly there was the sound of movement from inside the house. His ears told him: along the passageway ahead of him, not up the stairs, no — ground floor, rear. The kitchen or the scullery, whatever it was they had back there. And the sound was followed by a cry, a kind of yelp, and then a man's voice moaning. There was a long silence. Then the muffled noise of movement again.

Before he realised what he had done, Wayne had reached through the broken glass, turned the knob of the Yale and stepped over the shards inside the doorway. He was shuffling his way in the gloom. He registered a tiled hallway, the bottom of a huge carved wooden staircase, and moved down the hallway towards the rear of the house. He registered that the smell of burned bacon was stronger here. He could hear voices, but he could not make out what they were saying. Perhaps they were both hurt. Perhaps they both needed help. There was a doorway at the end of the passage, with light showing under the door. He crept a little closer. He had his hand on the door knob. He could hear a man's voice, it sounded like he was asking a question, but Wayne could not make out the words. The man spoke again, the same words a little louder this time. There was a roaring-hissing sound and then a long scream.

Whatever was going on in there Wayne realised he should have nothing to do with it, that he really should get out. Wayne backed away from the door, but as he did so his heel scraped the skirting board. The noise was not loud, but immediately the door at the end of the passage opened, bathing Wayne in light. The smell of burned bacon wafted over him hot and nauseating. Wayne caught a glimpse of a man who appeared to be tied into a chair, he had no shirt and his chest was a mass of blood and black burnt flesh. His head was lolling forward. To one side of the chair stood a man wearing khaki shorts and clutching a blow torch. Wayne backed away, his eyes wide when another man appeared in the doorway, blocking his view. Wayne barely had time to register that the man was levelling a shotgun at him when the shotgun barked.

Wayne flew backwards along the hall, hit the wall and slid down at an angle. His eyes were still open, but he was dead before he reached the floor.

The man next to the chair put down the blow torch and pushed past the man with the shotgun into the hall. Placing his hand on the wall, over the deep gouges caused by the shotgun blast he leaned over Wayne's body, staring down at the bloody mess as it settled. He stepped away from the spreading pool of blood. After a moment he turned to the man with the gun.

"Shit," was all he said. But he said it in German.

"Shit," echoed the other, but he said it in Spanish.

Years later...

Second of March 2000. I remember it well. I have good reason to. We were in *The White Lion*. I finished my coffee. Jack, my husband, had finished his glass of wine some time ago. The others were determined to make a night of it. It was not a party exactly, just a group of friends having the first drink of the new century together. It was a kind of belated New Year gathering. After all, the century was barely two months old. Just recently we'd been meeting up once a month. It was a fairly new departure really. We started celebrating with the election of the New Labour government, and it sort of carried on from there, but we'd all given a meeting at the end of January a miss as it was still too close to all the New Year shenanigans. With the Tories gone it was like a great weight lifted, we actually felt like going out for a drink, meeting friends. Even though we still had to live with the wreckage the Tories had created. And three years into the Labour term of office we still felt the same. We could still hum along to the song 'Things can only get better' with a clear conscience. We might have begun to feel that Labour was not the best government in the world, but we still felt very good about getting the Tories out, and for the moment that was good enough.

My husband is not a very political person, you understand. He's rather cynical. Politics to me is the art of the possible, but for him it is words, posturing, vote chasing. For him politicians, by and large, are professional liars. I understand him, I was once very like him. But I have become more of a political animal. I take it all very seriously. Even as a student I was into politics a little bit. I would say to him: 'I'm a journalist, words are my business, and I know a *scheister* when I hear one'. And he would say: 'Then you and the politicians are in the same business. Politicians, writers, journalists. You all make pictures with words. You all sell packages of lies pre-wrapped in words.'

I know he says that to wind me up. But what really winds me up is not that it simply isn't true, but that I know there is more than a grain of truth in it. I'm a member of the Labour Party — New Labour, that is. Jack would not join any Party. But that's OK with me. We get along just fine. Tolerance. That's the word. We have learned to tolerate each other's differences of opinion. And you know, if truth were told, I think we might even agree on the things we disagree about. Anyway, that night we were drinking with people who mainly also happened to be fellow Party members.

We had been there for a while, chatting about this and that. It wasn't crowded, so we lingered longer than we would normally. But then Jack's hip began to hurt. He didn't say anything, but I saw him shift his position in the chair and I knew he was suffering in silence. Jack had been a keen cyclist, a real sportsman. It had been normal for him to get up early on a Sunday morning, meet up with a couple of pals, and go off on a hundred mile round trip before lunch. Years ago he'd been part of the British cycling team at the Commonwealth Games in Jamaica. He had a collection of medals. But all that ended when he was knocked off his bike by a speeding police car. He had been in hospital for months with a shattered hip, and when he came out his cycling days were over. The police had paid him a small sum as compensation, but as Jack said, not only was the amount derisory, but how could you compensate someone for a thing like that?

Even though I was having a good time, I could see Jack probably wanted to go home. I finished my drink, and Jack, as if he was waiting for a signal, stood up and began to put on his coat. The others decided they were going on to *The Ajax*, to watch football on Sky TV. We gathered up hats, coats, bags and made our way outside. There was a brisk March wind. After a couple of minutes chatting on the pavement we split up with loud cheerios to go our separate ways. Jack and I headed round the back of the pub, past the bouncy castle, deserted in the darkness, to the car park.

He said: "You know it's only a matter of time before they knock this place down and turn it into a block of flats or a supermarket or something."

"Oh," I said. "And what makes you think that?"

"Stands to reason. Look, the car park is half empty. It's not doing good enough business to keep the brewery happy, you can be sure. They'll sell it off as land for development."

"Maybe not," I said. "It's such a nice place. You know, quiet. You can have a drink in peace here."

"That's what I'm saying. It's quiet. They won't be making enough…"

"Oh I hope not," I said, trying not to contradict him.

I drove slowly up past the fire station and the cinema, and then asked Jack if he would mind if I looked into a travel agent's window for a moment. I was bargain holiday hunting. I pulled over and parked opposite the Methodist Chapel. Jack came with me to the window, limping slightly. It was dark inside the shop, but the window display of brochures and posters, and the cards with the details of holidays currently on offer, was well lit. Jack said he wanted to go somewhere different this year. He rarely manages to get more than a few days off at a time, and he was tired of the same old holiday packages. I pointed to a picture of Italy, but he pointed at a brochure for Cyprus, and I thought that means he's probably already decided what he wants. I don't mind. From what I've read Cyprus is very nice, especially in the springtime. Mind, it would not be a bargain holiday. Cyprus would take some saving for. Arm in arm we went back to the car.

I was just about to get in when a poster at the newspaper shop across the street caught my eye. It read: *UK Returns General Pinochet.* I stood staring. My husband saw what I was looking at but did not seem to notice my reaction.

"It came on the news late this afternoon. A right old hoo-hah. Diplomats running about, statements flying. Didn't you hear about it? Come on...."

In the car I turned on the radio. We caught the news roundup.

...and finally, Spanish diplomats are tonight urgently seeking discussion with the British government about the return of General Pinochet to Chile. They are insisting that Britain has not honoured international law and that the General, who has been judged unfit to stand trial because of poor health, should still have faced extradition to Spain on charges of murder and torture. France, Belgium and Switzerland have also registered charges against the General. Sources close to Pinochet, who was arrested at a London hospital sixteen months ago while being treated for back problems, claimed that the ageing General Pinochet is still a great friend to Britain. The General had been a frequent visitor to Britain for nearly twenty years and is on very friendly terms with Baroness Thatcher. His supporters still maintain the General had diplomatic immunity and his arrest in Britain was illegal. However, a spokesman for the Chilean exile community in Britain criticised the British Home Secretary and expressed the hope that General Pinochet might still stand trial for his crimes when he returns to Chile. Former Prime Minister, Baroness Thatcher was quick to applaud the decision to release the General, and this evening said....

My husband turned off the radio very smartly.

"The un-dead speak."

"Well, it is after dark."

"But really, just when you think it's safe she pops up again."

"It was bad enough we had to listen to that bullying bitch when she was in office."

"Mrs Thatcher and General Pinochet.... last remnants of the vulture culture."

"You wish."

"Right. I wish."

13

"This story will run and run," I said. "I have a feeling."

"And I've learned to trust your feelings."

"Listen. An idea."

"What?"

"Is your hip hurting?"

"I could take a painkiller. Why?"

"I want to see something. Are you up for it?"

"Depends."

"A little business left over from my student days. Can you give me a few minutes?"

He knew it would be something political. I drove to the city centre. I'm sure he guessed where we were going long before we got there. We drove up Oxford Road, past the university buildings and into the city centre, we crossed Whitworth Street and turned across Canal Street, then down Charter Street. I pulled up across the street from the imposing eighteenth century building that housed the Chilean Consular offices.

From the face of the building remote CCTV cameras were trained on the crowd below. There were about forty people standing peacefully: women with children in push chairs, old men on sticks, students, young people in jeans and leather jackets. A few, mostly clutching roll-your-own cigarettes, wore the orange plastic bibs of the Socialist Workers Party. There were a sprinkling of placards. *Pinochet Mass Murderer. Pinochet Assassin. I am Torture Victim.* A few faces turned to look at us as we got out of the car.

Several policemen stood at the entrance to the Consulate, and another group stood at the corner watching the demonstrators. On the corner there was a police dog van and nearby were two mounted police. Jack said:

"I really don't want to stay too long Emma. All this makes me uncomfortable, if anything happens I can't run...."

"I know, Jack. I won't be long."

14

I was already heading towards the demonstration. Jack caught up with me only because a police sergeant blocked my path.

"And just where d'you think you're going?"

"Joining the demonstration, officer."

"Don't you think we got enough problems?"

"Your problems are your problems sergeant, but it's my right to demonstrate peacefully if I wish."

"With this rabble...."

"This is not Chile, sergeant, and the Tories are no longer in power."

"So?"

"So this is still a democracy. Just...."

"That's as may be, but any trouble...."

"I do hope you are not threatening me, officer."

My husband took a long look at the number on the sergeant's epaulette, and made sure the policeman saw him do it.

"Sergeant, servant of the public, unless you have good reason to detain us, stand aside please, and let the good citizen Emma Tulip pass."

The sergeant stood a fraction to one side. I pushed past him and headed for the demonstration.

"You see? If he had cut up rough," said Jack, "I couldn't run away.."

"I wouldn't want you to run away. He's a bloody fascist."

Jack laughed and put his arm around me. "I've noticed you don't blink when you face up to someone you think is a fascist."

"Good thing it doesn't happen too often."

"In animals not blinking is a sign of aggression."

"OK. OK. So I'm a swine sometimes. But if that's the only language he understands. What was he trying to do? Warn us off? Prevent us from joining a peaceful demonstration? Look. A demonstration, in a good and just cause. My God we haven't had one of these for such a long time. Takes me back a bit. Don't worry, we won't stay long."

Jack spotted someone he knew.

"Ah, *buenas noches señor....*" and he was shaking hands, chatting, dredging up the few bits of holiday Spanish he had retained. I will say that for Jack. He may not know much about foreign languages, but the few words he does know he makes work very hard for him. And besides, I thought, it will take his mind off the pain in his hip.

We stayed for about an hour, all the while I was moving about, shaking hands, chatting, chatting, chatting. It seemed like, one way or another, I knew about half the people in the demonstration. That's what comes of being a local journalist, I suppose. There was little doubt that everyone present thought General Pinochet should not have been released, that he was pretending to be ill, that he had pulled the wool over the eyes of Jack Straw. The cold March wind died down. And the sky, which had been threatening to go typically Manchester on us for most of the evening, finally clouded over completely. A light drizzle started. I knew the cold and the damp would make Jack's hip ache ferociously.

Jack was standing in a doorway. He saw me, shook hands with his friend and came towards me, limping heavily.

"Jack, good grief. You've been standing all this time. Why didn't you say?"

"I did, sweetheart, I did." He pulled up the collar of my coat against the rain.

"But you could have sat in the car, at least...."

"And miss all this networking? So who did you meet?"

"Just about everybody on the left hereabouts I think. And you?"

"I met Costas."

"Greek?"

"Cypriot actually."

"Owner of the kebab shop?"

"No. Runs a specialist Greek travel agency."

"And?"

"Well, I was just having a word with him... that's all...."

16

"Oh! Costas the communist?"

"Commie Costas, that's him."

"Right. Very nice fellah."

"Anyway, he says he can do us a great deal on a summer holiday."

"Ah, so that's why you are not complaining about standing around in the cold."

"Abso-bloody-lutely."

"Also I bumped into Jaime and his wife Maria-Dolores. They say they are writing a book about Pinochet, trying to keep the story in the public eye and fill everybody in on the history of it all."

"Well, he is a university lecturer. That's what they do — write books."

"I'm looking forward to it. He writes very well."

"He has an axe to grind."

"Well, after what Pinochet did to his family I'm not surprised."

We crossed the street, to the car. Jack waved to the crowd. A couple of hands fluttered in return. As we moved off I noticed the police on the corner looking down the next street. Something was happening that we could not see. We drove slowly towards them, turning the corner. At the far end of the street we could see a small crowd milling around in the road under the yellow street lights. People were running from the shadows to join them. They were waving placards. I could just make out: *Pinochet innicent: friend all poor people*s. And as we drove closer I could see there was some kind of a fight. Someone was lying on the road. I put my hand on the horn and drove fast towards them, as if I intended to run them all down, then I stood on the brake and we came to a squealing halt. Jack and I flung the car doors wide and made it look as if we were planning to join the fight. The group scattered into the alleys and shadows, leaving just a couple of people behind. One man leaned against a lamp-post breathing heavily. In the gutter another man slumped, groaning and clutching his face. A third lay in a dark spreading pool. In the road

17

was a placard: *He kill my family*. Behind me I heard the clatter of running feet and a dog barking as the police arrived. A policewoman knelt by the man lying in the road. After a moment she began to give mouth to mouth resuscitation. A mounted police officer rode up, the horse hooves clattering on the street. He looked down from the saddle and spoke into a collar mike.

"Control, this is Fox-Trot-Delta. Send an ambulance immediately. Corner of Owlet Lane and Back Piccadilly."

"Are you OK?" I asked.

"Saw them off at least," said Jack, breathing heavily.

"Who were they?"

"Dunno. I'd say this was the counter demonstration — friends of the General maybe. And they seem to have caught a couple of stragglers from the group at the Consulate. But it could be the other way round. These could be the General's supporters caught by the opposition...."

I could see the policewoman's face as she struggled to get the man on the floor to start breathing again. A policeman arrived on foot from a nearby side alley, knelt down on the road beside the policewoman and began heart massage.

"I think we just witnessed a murder."

I took Jack by the elbow and walked him back to the car. He leaned against it, looking over my shoulder at the scene on the road.

"Are you all right?" I said. "You look as if you are about to pass out."

"Yes, fine. Just a little shocked. That's all."

"Is the pain bad?"

"Very."

I began to rummage about in the glove compartment for Jack's painkillers. And as I found them I looked up, through the windscreen, to an alley way. A man stood there in the shadow, watching. He was small, undersized, dressed in a raincoat with the collar turned up. He was very still, watching events in the roadway intently. But as

I looked at him he turned away from the scene in the road. The light fell on his face. I registered that his face was old, very old and lined. He was wearing glasses with thick lenses. But then I caught my breath. I recognised him. He raised his finger to his lips as if to say: 'Shhhh'. And then, with a leering smile he lowered the finger from his lips, pointed it at me as if it were a gun, and the thumb moved like the hammer on a pistol. I gulped. He ducked into the shadows of the alley and was gone. He had recognised me. There was no doubt.

For a moment I could not move. My heart pounded and I just wanted to scream. But then a policewoman came over to the car.

"Excuse me," she said, taking out her notebook. "Would you mind if I took your names please?"

My husband answered.

"Emma Tulip and Jack Emmet."

"Thank you. And can I ask you to stay here for a little while. We will need to take a statement."

"Certainly. We'll wait."

"I'm sorry, but this could turn out to be serious. It may be a while."

"We understand."

My husband turned to look at me.

"How about you? You don't look too good."

"Me? Yes. I'm OK. I shouldn't have dragged you along here. I'm sorry." I handed him the tablets.

"An apology? You must be shaken up worse than I thought."

"No it's not that. It's just that.... well, Chile. I'm connected to all this in a weird way."

Frowning, Jack popped a painkiller into his mouth. "Connected? Connected to the punch-up? How?"

"Not the punch up, no. To Chile. To the General."

"To Pinochet?"

"Yes."

"Not a distant relative of his are you?"

"No nothing like that."

19

"What then?"

"A long time ago. Before I met you."

"Before I went 'hip'?"

This was his little joke. A nice play on words when you hear it the first time.

"Yes. A long while before you went 'hip'."

"From your student days?"

"No after that."

"A story for the paper?"

"It was a story. Yes... sort of...."

"You're not going to tell me General Pinochet is an old boyfriend, are you? My God, you don't have history as a closet fascist?"

"No. Don't be silly. Nothing like that."

He opened the car door and I got in. He went round to the other side. We sat in silence for a moment. He nodded at the group huddled round the figure on the floor.

"I don't think that poor bloke's going to make it."

"Doesn't look like it."

"So, you had a brush with Chile and the General."

"Yes. I... well, it was a long time ago and Chile is a long way away, but sometimes history just reaches out and grabs you, you know?"

"What's the story then?"

"It's not something I think about very often. At least, I try not to."

"Sounds like something I should know about though."

"Yes. Yes. I should explain. I have always meant to tell you about it.... this just brought it all back to me."

"Well, we have to wait here anyway, so why not?"

"To make a statement. Yes. Just in case...."

"Well, come on then, if it's a story you'd better tell it."

We sat quietly for a moment. I was desperately trying to order my thoughts. I went back. Back to a cold February night in 1985, back to things I had put behind me and things I would much rather forget. My husband, patient as always, waited.

"It all began," I said, "when Clifford rang me. I thought

20

at first it was a Valentine's Day message. I was a bit like that in those days."

Chronology: 1970

By 1970 Chile had been ruled as a civilian democracy for 162 years. The country was widely considered to be one of the most stable of the South American states. Nevertheless, 40% of Chileans suffered from malnutrition; 33% of all deaths were children; 3% of the population owned 40% of the nation's wealth; and 50% of the working population earned less than 10% of the national wealth. In 1970, after serving twenty-five years as a democratically elected Senator, Marxist leader Salvador Allende sought election to the post of Chilean President. In opening his Presidential Election Campaign in the summer of 1970, he said: 'Chile is rich in natural resources. We could be a rich country. Instead we are poor. For more than four centuries, our most valuable natural resources have been owned by foreigners — first the Spanish, then the English, and now the North Americans. The profits taken from Chile by the US copper companies are equivalent to the entire present total of our wealth — that is the same as a whole Chile lost to Chileans forever.' This was to be Allende's fourth attempt at election to President.

Jaime Perez-Cervera & Maria-Dolores Jamon,
Augusto: The Little Book of the General

Back into the past....

The phone had not rung for several days, possibly even a couple of weeks, so I was very surprised. At first I could only look at it. I was unable or unwilling to move. But old reflexes took over. Though I was wary of the thing, I answered. My first thought was, it's a Valentine's Day message. It was Clifford. He seemed bright and cheerful. And I still thought, it could be a Valentine.

"Clifford, long time no-see."

"Yeah I been a very busy boy."

"As usual."

"I've got something for you."

"Whatever it is, the chances are I don't want it."

"No seriously, I've got something that will interest you."

"Clifford, we've been through this before. Nothing you've got interests me."

"You know that's not true."

"That is your masculine pride talking, Clifford."

"Nah, you're just determined to make me try harder."

"I don't want to get into that again, Clifford."

"OK, let's just say that for the moment I accept your temporary indisposition. But anyway, it's not that."

"Not what?"

"You know."

"Unfortunately I do. When a bloke says..."

"It's a story."

"Aha. I'm out of the business, Clifford. You know, I was retired... or haven't you heard?"

"I heard. But you're too young to retire."

"Flatterer."

"I can't talk now."

"Are you at the office darling?"

"Of course, and the Chief Superintendent's buzzing around. I'll meet you at three, at the Domino."

"But I'm not in the business anymore."

"Yeah, you said. But this is just too good to miss."

I put the phone down. Part work, part date. It was always like that with Clifford. There was always that little edge of interest. I had first met Clifford Usher when I was covering local crime stories for the *Gazette*. Clifford was straight out of police training college, much younger than me, but he had started trying to get into my underwear right away. Not in an obvious way, mind, but he made sure I noticed him. Eventually he succeeded. We had a sort of thing for a while, just briefly. But, too many problems. It didn't work. Apart from all the obvious problems, a copper and a journalist? It was a bad mix. Neither of us was ever at home, and when we were, we were usually exhausted. We hardly saw each other. It didn't last long. We both regretted it, but it was not a bad split, and we still kept in touch from time to time. So what was this about? He gave me no clue.

I found Clifford in the Domino. He was as handsome as ever, reading a copy of *The South Manchester Echo*, sat in front of the fish tank. As I approached he looked as if he had a little halo of neon tetras.

"Why are you wearing sunglasses Clifford?"

"I don't want to be seen, do I?"

"I get it. You're CID: Copper in Disguise... Or is that Clifford in disguise?"

"Yeah, old joke. Very unfunny."

"Very effective, Clifford. Uniform trousers, blue shirt, black shiny shoes. Dark glasses... indoors... in February... that's quite a disguise."

The waitress approached shuffling her feet, wiping her nose on the back of her hand and clutching a cloth that looked as if its previous owner was a car mechanic.

"Two frothy coffees please," said Clifford.

"Hang on, Clifford, I might have wanted something else."

"Nah, you ain't gonna drink it. It's just for the look of the thing, isn't it?"

"Oh, like part of the disguise."

23

"That's it." Clifford seemed very pleased with himself.

"I got my promotion last week."

"Congratulations Clifford. One of the first, you are."

"Nah, the last in my class to get stripes. And we know why that is."

"True. You deserved stripes years ago... mostly on the arse."

"Didn't know you were into that kind of thing."

"Don't get your hopes up, Clifford."

"No. Truth is.... everything's different now, Emma. I got married."

"Wonders will never cease. Well congratulations again Clifford."

"And a nipper on the way too."

"They connected, these two events?"

"Possibly," said Clifford, smiling.

"You don't waste time do you?"

"I try not to." The coffee arrived. I took a sip.

"You're right Clifford, I won't be drinking this. So come on, what's the story?"

"Oh, it's a peach."

"Tell."

"Well, you covered a story a few years back, so you probably know more about this than me. It was a case where a kid was delivering groceries or something, disturbed a robbery at a big house... remember?"

"Vividly. Druids Hill. 1975. Very nasty business altogether. Tortured the tenant with a blowtorch, then killed the kid and the tenant with a shotgun."

"Yeah. Nobody could work it out. Nothing taken from the house — not that there was anything worth nicking by the looks of things. No clues. No motive. Nothing."

"They'd turned the place over though."

"Oh yeah. Left a right mess. But nothing for forensic to get hold of."

"So eventually the investigation ran out of steam."

"Sort of, yeah."

"Sort of?"

"Yeah, something like that."

"What sort of something."

"Difficult to say exactly, you know."

"Well, difficult such as?"

"Such as this. Last week we had a missing person turn up. Disappeared shortly after the big house job. A well educated geezer, very respectable."

"So can you fit him up for the farmhouse job? Finally. After all this time? What is it? Ten years?"

"No, hang on. I don't fit up nobody for nothing."

"True. Unfair comment. I apologise."

"And anyway, that's not the point."

"Well what is the point?"

"See, the bloke that turned up last week... he's turned up all right, but he's turned up dead."

"Well, that's most unfortunate Clifford, but it could happen to anybody... in fact you'd be surprised."

"Stop being a smart arse and listen. They found him floating in Dublin ferry port."

"Drowned?"

"No. Slightly dead before he hit the water. Shot."

"Dublin drug wars?"

"Maybe. Maybe not."

"And why should this interest me?"

"Because Irish ballistics has got a brand new computer, and their brand new computer says this geezer was shot in the chest by the same gun used at the Druids Hill job. They made a match with the marks on the pellets and the pellet spread."

"Well, sadly Irish ballistics has more experience than most with that sort of thing."

"No question."

"So who was he?"

"Ah, that's the interesting part. Clifford sipped his coffee and grimaced.

"Cor! Somebody should do this place. This ain't coffee it's..."

"Clifford, are you going to tell me who he was or what?"

"Yeah. You might have known him. A local guy called David Agard."

"Can't say I recall him. Where did he work? Did he work?"

"Oh yeah, he worked. He worked for us. Right here in the local nick. Which is why I thought you might have met him. He was our senior computer officer. A real wizard, apparently."

"Police?"

"No, a civilian. Nearly police."

"Well, he's not nearly dead, is he?"

"No, he's ever so more than slightly very dead."

"Was he on the farmhouse case?"

"Not strictly speaking. As a civilian he wasn't. But he was part of the station team, so he was part of the technical back up for the investigation. He handled all the information, collation, retrieval. All that stuff."

"And why did he disappear?"

"Nobody knows."

"And you think there's a connection?"

"I thought you'd retired. You're interested aren't you? I was right."

"Maybe I'm intrigued, that's all."

Chronology: 1970

Between 1964 and 1970 the CIA had spent more than $20,000,000 on anti-Marxist propaganda to prevent Allende being elected to the Presidency. In the run-up to the 1970 Chilean Presidential elections, at the instigation of US President Richard Nixon, National Security Council Chairman Henry Kissinger and the CIA spent another $500,000,000 dollars on its anti-Allende campaign, channelling the money into Chile via ITT, Pepsi and the copper mining giants Kennecot and Anaconda. In spite of this, Allende won the election by the narrow margin of 39,000 votes.

The CIA, having failed to promote a military coup to prevent Allende's election to President, arranged the assassination of General Rene Schneider, Allende's main democratic supporter within the Chilean military. Two days later the Chilean Congress voted to confirm Allende's democratic election victory by a vote of 153 to 35, and Allende, the world's first freely elected Marxist President, was officially inaugurated. He had a coalition government of fifteen members, only three of whom were Communists and only four of whom came from his own Chilean Socialist Party.

Jaime Perez-Cervera & Maria-Dolores Jamon,
Augusto: The Little Book of the General

On the way home from the Domino I bought copies of all the daily newspapers, and when I got in I fed Maggie and Adolf, my two goldfish, put food down for Beastly, the cat, and then listened to the radio news. There was nothing about the body in Dublin harbour. I waited for the evening news on TV, but there was nothing there either, so I went for a wander in the park. And I remember thinking Clifford, you have a nice smile, a nice manner, good sense of humour. Pity it didn't work out. But anyway, now he was a sergeant, married, child on the way, it just would not be fair to.... Well, I caught myself thinking those things, and feeling those feelings, and I wondered if that wasn't what Clifford wanted me to do. He's a smart bugger is Clifford, and if it will help him get what he wants, he'll turn on the charm. And just because I'm paranoid it doesn't mean I'm wrong, does it? It was nice that Clifford had finally got his promotion — he'd done the exam and waited long enough, but he had been passed-over for promotion several times. And the longer he had waited the more obvious it had become. Everyone knew why he was being passed over. Nobody said anything, of course. Well they wouldn't. Couldn't. But it must have been very frustrating for Clifford. As far as I could tell he was a good copper. He did his job, didn't fit up anybody for crimes they hadn't done, didn't take bribes. But that didn't mean he was well liked by his work mates, though I think they all felt they should have coppers like Clifford around. Mind, this was in the days when the local Chief Constable was on first name terms with God, when coppers regularly used the company car to fetch the family groceries, when drug money was sloshing around the nick like some kind of silent tidal wave.

A large slice of the local population trusted Clifford, he steadied the younger coppers, calmed the hooligans. Any trouble in Moss Side, any clients from that side of town needed talking to Clifford was the one they called for. And the black kids, although they didn't entirely trust him — 'raz klat gon Babylon' they'd say — knew they'd get a fairer deal from Clifford than they would from most of the other coppers. In an odd kind of way the police needed him. But that only made his failure to get promotion even more obvious.

There had been a clean up. Of sorts. The Chief Constable's Hot Line to God hit all the newspapers and he suddenly got 'promotion' to a 'non-executive' post advising the Home Office. Several coppers were investigated by Internal Affairs, and suspended for fiddling their expenses. The serious Crimes Squad, which had a disastrous record of absolutely zero busts in nearly ten years, was disbanded and the coppers were all returned to normal duties. One or two members, guessing what was on the way, had already transferred to other forces. It did not amount to much, but, with all the to-ing and fro-ing, I assumed a few posts became vacant and Clifford had finally got his promotion out of it.

I wandered around Fog Lane park a couple of times, avoiding the dog-crap and the flooded bits. It was a scabby little park, really, but I liked it. I often went there. I was very fond of the animal enclosure — they had goats and sheep and ponies and donkeys, guinea fowl, all just wandering around. I used to find it very calming to watch the animals, especially in the spring, when the goats and sheep had young. It was always great fun to watch the kids and the lambs gambolling around the place, playing king of the castle. All gone now of course. The council couldn't afford the upkeep and local people couldn't keep it going on a voluntary basis. Each time I went there I wondered how much longer we would have the park for, how long would it be before Mrs Thatcher or one of her vegetable cabinet suggested a scheme to privatise public parks, and sell them off cheaply to their pals to build golf courses. Why golf courses? Well there's no point building houses or factories, I hear the fat cats cry: there's no work for the factories and no money to buy the houses. So why not build a golf course? Private, naturally.

In one corner of the park there was a football match. They were playing on Astroturf, which is a mean and nasty surface, so I'm told, if you fall and get cut. The plastic grass cuts you open and the sand filler gets into the wounds so they don't heal for weeks, just ooze pus. Still Astroturf saves money on ground-keepers because it doesn't need trimming, and that's the main thing isn't it, never mind the players. This lot seemed to be doing more arguing than playing. One of them had taken a tumble and the others, ignoring the poor bugger who was rolling around screaming and clutching his knee were shouting, gesturing, pushing and shoving. Young Arabs, mostly by the look of it. Eventually the one on the floor seemed to lose interest in the game and limped off.

I kept well away from the footballers and headed for the pond. It was still possible to see wild birds on the pond. And true enough there were some canada geese with this year's goslings almost as big as the adults, some mallards, some ordinary white geese, a moorhen and nearly fully grown chicks, and over in the shallows at the other end of the pool there was a heron. The heron was big and grey and intent on his fishing. I'd heard several local people saying the heron had eaten the goldfish out of their back garden ponds. If he had, he didn't look guilty about it. To a heron lunch is lunch, and that's the end of it. I saw a teal on this pond, once, and a mandarin duck.

I found a bench and perched on the one remaining unbroken slat. I had questions revolving in my head, emerging, taking shape. Firstly, I could not help wondering, why Clifford was feeding me this info? What did he think I could do with this? I'd said I was retired. Retired hurt, more like. I lost my job when my newspaper was bought out by a millionaire. He owned several national papers, and really all he was doing was buying up the competition in order to close us down. A very effective way of dealing with the opposition, and one that democracy still allows. A few of us journos had been taken on by the rivals, one or two went off to London clutching a portfolio of stories never to be seen again. But I didn't manage to get a thing. Apart from a large redundancy payment, that is. And that was nearly gone.

For the last few months I'd been living on the redundancy money, and eking out a living doing book reviews, interviewing local celebrities, running around as a stringer, covering stories where it wasn't worthwhile to send a 'proper' reporter down from London. It paid the bills, just, but things were getting very tight. So maybe this story from Clifford was a bit of a gift after all. But what puzzled me was: why, if this body was found last week, and had now been identified, was there nothing in the news about it?

When I got home the phone was ringing. It was Clifford.

"So what do you think?"

"Why me Clifford? You could leak this to the nationals, get yourself a nice little back-hander."

"Yeah, but they'd track it back to me in the end. This way, you get a good story."

"And you can say, but she's a local, of course she'd find out."

"Exactly."

30

"Clever Clifford"

"Glad you think so."

"And where do I start?"

"No idea."

"Did Agard have a wife?"

"Haven't got a clue."

"So that's as good a place as anywhere then."

"Right."

"And what is it I'm looking for exactly?"

"The story, basically. The story."

"Intriguing."

"Yeah. You've got to think about the angles on this one. I mean, about the original murder at the farmhouse. Was Agard's disappearance connected in some way? Where was he all that time? I mean, ten years. Why does he reappear now? Why is he dead? Why was he killed with the same gun."

"Yes, thank you Clifford. I have my own questions."

"Only trying to be helpful."

"Clifford, one last question. Instinct. My instinct tells me. Something isn't quite right... why was there nothing in the news about this body?"

"Dunno... but you're right. I can't put my finger on it, but there's just no urgency here. No case conference, no contact with the Irish forensic people, nobody's doing anything. It's just a feeling, but I reckon without some kind of outside interest this investigation won't get anywhere."

"And that's where I come in."

"Only if you want."

"Sounds dodgy, Clifford. You're not dropping me in it are you."

"Nah. You might take a little heat, that's all."

"Yeah, and you might get promoted to Inspector."

"You reckon?"

"Not a hope."

"That's what I think."

Chronology: 21 December 1970

Over the first year of Allende's Presidency, while the coalition government struggled to master an inherited foreign debt of over $3,000,000,000 [the second highest per capita debt in the world at that time], it increased the minimum wage by 35% and launched a programme to provide free milk daily to children and pregnant or nursing mothers. In addition to the 8,500,000 acres of land nationalised by the previous government, the coalition proposed to nationalise a further 3,500,000 acres of privately owned land that was inefficiently farmed.

As a result of these measures, in the following year unemployment dropped from 8.3% to 3.9%, inflation fell from 35% to 22%, child mortality dropped by 11%, the Chilean GNP tripled and industrial production rose by 14.6%. In the municipal elections of April 1971 Allende's Popular Unity Coalition improved its vote from 36% to 49.7%.

Jaime Perez-Cervera & Maria-Dolores Jamon
Augusto: The Little Book of the General

The possibility of a Mrs Agard. That seemed like a good place to start. But how to find her? Just in case, I thought, I should look in the phone book. No dice. Where had she lived in 1975? At that time her husband was in a good job, true. But as a civilian he was probably not eligible for a police-house, even though he worked for the police. So a trip to the Town Hall was called for, and a quick flip through the electoral register.

The bus was crowded with students. I didn't mind the students, but they all seemed to have hacking, barking coughs. It was like being in a seal colony. I felt sorry for them really. The kind of thing that gets palmed off on them as an education, even as a degree, was unthinkable in my day. Now it was just a business and they were just clients. I think they were probably vaguely aware that they were getting something substandard, but what could they do about it?

For me the Town Hall was always a pleasure to visit, and afterwards I had promised myself a real coffee at the

San Marco cafe. Some people say the Town Hall is gloomy, but I love the arches and the stairways, the high carved wooden doors and the mosaic floors. The porter told me the electoral registers were kept in a special store in the basement — which I already knew. And then he ushered me down a winding stone staircase and along a narrow corridor into a dimly lit room the size of a football pitch. The Clerk to the Electoral Registrar came out from behind his desk, and moved through the gloom towards us. The porter faded away.

"Our local electoral rolls are not computerised," the Clerk said. "They are exactly what they sound like."

He gestured at the room. My eyes were getting used to the lighting — or rather to the lack of lighting. The electoral registers looked like giant lavatory rolls on spindles, set in carved and very elegant wooden frames at about waist height. They stood in neat rows down the room.

"One of my predecessors devised these rather wonderful stands for the registers and the Electoral Registrar had several dozen of them built to order. They say they will computerise all this one day, but somehow I just can't see it. We may be archaic but at least we have a system that works. It takes time though. It does take time."

He seemed pleased with the idea.

"Which is the current roll?"

"That would be this one." He gestured to the roll nearest the desk. "It is manual access only, I'm afraid. You stand here, and then you look down here. Now turn this handle, the drum rotates. The names are listed alphabetically by surname. Might I suggest that you don't turn the handle too fast? Or you will overshoot your mark. It is currently rewound to the letter A."

"And then the next roll back in time would be..."

"That's right, the roll standing just behind you, and so on back down the rows until you get to our oldest roll. But you will need to fill out a form if you want to look at anything other than the current roll. Call me if you need assistance." He returned to his desk.

Mrs Agard was not on the current roll, and I had to negotiate access to previous rolls. Nobody had looked at them for years. I had to cover my face with a hankie, they were so dusty. Anyway, there was no point going through them all: I cut straight to the roll for 1975. Bingo. David Agard and Muriel Agard, 24 Willow Way, Withens Residential Estate. And then I thought, so you found where they used to live. So what? That is just the starting point. I blew the dust out of my nose, thanked the Clerk and went to find a bus. I had forgotten all about the promise I had made myself of a decent cup of coffee in the Cafe San Marco.

The Withens Residential Estate consisted of nice neat redbrick houses with nice neat drives, nice neat gardens with nice neat lawns and nice neat trees and shrubs. Not a weed in sight. Not a toy abandoned. Not a garage door left open. Not a car parked crookedly. Everybody seemed to be in their late twenties with a cat and 2.5 kids. Or was that 2.5 cats and a kid? Never could remember which way round. As I walked up Willow Way a husband sat in his car talking on a car phone. It was the first time I had seen a car phone. A woman stood in her front porch smoking a cigarette, casting furtive glances alternately back into the house and then down the road. I doubted that any of these people had lived here when Agard and his family were in residence, but you never knew for sure until you knocked on a few doors and asked a few questions. But after a few doors I was almost certain — almost. The last house I tried had a little blue rinse lady sitting in the window. She met me at the door.

"I saw you working your way along the street and I wondered how long it would be before you got to me. What are you selling? Insurance? Time-share apartments on the Algarve? Whatever it is I don't want any."

"I'm looking for someone."

"Aren't we all, dear? What have they done? Something nice and juicy, I hope. A murder? Bigamy?"

"Nothing so bold. I'm a solicitor's clerk. I'm trying to

trace a Mrs Agard. It's an inheritance. I'm just trying to pass on the money. It'll go begging if I can't find her."

"The Agards! I remember them, of course. I'm sure I can be of some assistance. Well, look, I'm just about to put the kettle on. Why don't you have a cup of tea, at least, dear. Then we can chat."

"Cup of tea would be very welcome."

She ushered me into her kitchen, put the kettle on and passed a plate of digestive biscuits across the table. She put a set of floral place mats on the table, followed by a tea service with pink and green flowers and gold edging to everything. She poured pale tea, splashed sterilised milk in a swirling stain, and then finally ladled six heaped spoons of white sugar into her cup. She sipped the tea without tasting it, leaving bright lipstick on the gold rim.

"Now what was it you were saying dear?"

I explained again that I was trying to track down the Agard family because a relative in Australia had died recently and they had come into some money. She brushed away biscuit crumbs from around her mouth.

"Yes, I recollect now. He worked for the police. Such a nice young family... but something went wrong there. Very wrong. It was all mysterious, of course. I don't know anything for certain. But I'd say he went off the rails or took a mistress or she took to drink. Something like that. Stress, probably. He couldn't cope, maybe. You hear such a lot of that these days."

"What happened? Did they move away?"

"The insurance policy matured did it, dear?"

"No," I said. "I told you, it's an inheritance."

"Oh, right. You did say... well, look, I think he ran away. And she moved out shortly afterwards."

"Maybe there was a temporary separation. Maybe they sorted things out and got together again later. You don't remember where they went, do you?"

"My poor departed husband used to say I have a memory like a steel trap. Once it's in there, that's where it stays. I sit here and I watch the street, you see. There's nothing else for me to do since my husband passed on. All the comings and goings. If you want to know what's going on around here... I know everything... everything that's fit to be known, and a great deal that isn't too."

"So where did they go?"

"That I don't know. We weren't on speaking terms. Not really. You know how it is; there's some people you speak to, and others you just nod to."

"But?"

"But the removals van was local, dear. That I do know. It had a local phone number and the name Murphy's on the side. At first I thought they were delivering potatoes."

We sat drinking tea and nibbling biscuits for another half hour, but that was really all she knew. She wanted to make a fresh pot of her weak tea, but I made my apologies, blaming my boss. She said: "You must come again, dear, it has been so nice to have a visitor."

She stood in her front window and waved to me until I reached the corner.

Chronology: 11 July 1971

Kennecot and Anaconda, the giant US owned copper mining companies, had planned to expand Chilean ore production by 355,000 tons per year. The US owned mines in Chile already produced vast profits, almost all of which were exported to the US rather than reinvested or spent in Chile. Kennecot's El Tenniente mine [the world's largest underground copper mine] produced an annual profit of 34.8%, compared with an average of less than 10% on Kennecot's investments in the rest of the world. Anaconda's Chuquicamata mine [the world's largest open cast copper mine] produced an annual profit of 20.2% compared with an average of 3.5% on the company's other investments world-wide. Less than 20% of Chilean copper production was actually in Chilean hands.

Now, in line with policies first proposed by the Christian Democratic Party and supported by most of the Chilean political leadership [including the opposition], Allende announced proposals to nationalise all US owned copper mines in Chile. This was in line with, and based on, the

UN Declaration of Principles, which holds that the natural wealth and riches of a people should be controlled and developed for the well being and development of that people and their state.

Jaime Perez-Cervera & Maria-Dolores Jamon
Augusto: The Little Book of the General

I was determined to get down to finding Mrs Agard, but I was having problems with my landlord. About a year ago I had complained that there was water running down the wall of my kitchen every time it rained. The whole wall was damp. I asked him to look at the guttering and the rendering on the side of the house. He did nothing. Everything in my cupboards started to go mouldy. I wrote to him again and asked him if he wanted me to get the work done and take the cost out of the rent. Next thing I knew, he had put the house up for sale, and I had a letter telling me I had to get out within three months. I took legal advice and refused to move. But I had a steady stream of people coming to the house with a clerk from the estate agent.

At first I thought, well, it is his house he can sell it if he wants, and if he is selling it with tenants then he will be selling it at a loss. But then, during one of these visits, I asked one of the estate agents' clerks and she said: "He's advertising it as vacant possession."

So I had to ring the estate agent and tell them that I was a tenant, with a rent book and a standing order at the bank, and that I had no plans to move out.

"But he told us very clearly. He said you were a friend, minding the property for him, and that you would move out as soon as it was sold."

"No. I am not his friend. Definitely not."

"And how long have you lived there, d'you say?"

"Several years — and I have bank records proving rent payments for the whole of my tenancy."

"But he told us, quite clearly that you had just moved in and that you were merely house sitting for him, to prevent squatters and that sort of thing."

"Perhaps you would prefer to talk to my solicitor about this?"

The estate agent promised to look into it and muttered something about the landlord telling porkies. Which just about summed it up, I thought. At the end of the day I still had a home to go to, I still had running water. Only, the water was running down my kitchen wall.

Anyway, I finally managed to put in some work on the Agards. I thought, I'll start with the removals people. Removals people never go very far, in one way. Murphy's Removals was a local firm. They were listed in the phone book. I spoke to a friendly receptionist called Abida and arranged a time to visit the office.

Murphy's Removal Specialists [Local and International] No Load Too Small, No Journey Too Far, turned out to be a family company housed in a long green shed in a court-yard behind a row of shops on Copson Street. Outside the front office was a tall plastic bin full of empty vodka bottles.

Abida who was dressed in a bright two-tone green cos-tume, gold platform heels, long purple nails and orange streaks in her hair was very helpful.

"I'm running this place at the moment. I do everything. Except drive the truck. That I would never do."

"Is the boss away?"

"Away? Er.... yes.... On business."

"I saw the bottles on the way in."

"Mr Murphy is sometimes an unhappy man."

"He must be a *very* unhappy man."

"Indeed. He has his reasons."

"I'm sure."

"And perhaps if he drank less he would be even more unhappy."

"Perhaps."

"Now how can I help you?"

"It is normal in these cases," I said, putting a ten pound note on the high desk, "to offer a discretionary award — a search fee."

That did the trick. I was invited round the front desk to stand with Abida in front of a big green filing cabinet.

"So what exactly would you want?"

"Just one piece of information. Where did the Agard family go when they left the Withens Estate?"

"And that's all."

"Absolutely."

"Good," she said pocketing my ten pound note. "This will pay for my Line Dancing class."

"Your what?"

"Texas Line Dancing."

"Never heard of it. What do you do?"

"You all stand in a line and dance the same dance steps. I go every week."

"I see."

"Trust me, it's going to be very big."

She riffled through the old filing cards.

"Ugh! Nobody's looked at these records in years. I have to go slowly, you understand, to protect my fingernails. A broken nail is the last thing I want. Appearance is very important in my line of work. Ah..."

She produced a file card and holding it at the very tips of her fingers she handed it to me.

"Keep that if you want. No point me trying to maintain decent records if he's gonna do himself in with drink, is there? I can't see the business lasting more than a few months."

"Will the children take over?"

"Pah! His children? They know only how to spend his money. They don't have a clue about work. They have no interest in this work."

"Time to find a new job, maybe."

"I reckon so. If there were any to find."

"What about your family? Could they help?"

"My family? Not a good idea."

"Well, if I hear of anything, any suitable work, I'll let you know."

"Oh would you? That's very kind. Reception work would

39

be just fine. I think I have a professional calling for it, you know."

On the street I looked at the card. I stared hard at it. I even raised an eyebrow. This change of address must have been quite a shock.

It took me a while to find Mrs Agard. Having an address on a filing card is one thing. Trying to actually locate the place in a rabbit warren of ancient back alleys and paved courtyards was entirely another matter. I'd been to this area before — several times — but it was not a part of town I regularly frequented. And if I had the choice I would not come here at all. It was one of those back-to-back areas that went up in the spaces between the factories in old east Manchester. The factory owners reckoned it was better to have their workers close at hand, but the results were not pretty. It was one of a row of six identically gloomy, soot-stained houses, set in a dark paved court just wide enough to hang out the washing on a Monday. And facing it was a row of six identical houses. There were no trees or bushes in the court, and no through road. This was a back alley with a vengeance.

I thumped the knocker and waited. It was a while before a woman I took to be some sort of a nurse opened the door.

"Does a Mrs Agard live here?"

"Are you Social Services? You'd better come in. She's out the back getting some air."

The nurse ushered me down a long dark hallway that smelled of cabbage, through a scullery, and out into a yard paved with blue engineering bricks. The end of the yard was blocked off by the steep brick face of a factory wall. I looked around and noted that nothing, absolutely nothing, was growing there. Mrs Agard was sitting in the shade. But then, everything was in the shade here. She wore dark glasses and a head scarf. She held a walking stick.

"She tires easily," the nurse said.

"What's wrong with her?"

"I just told you. She tires easily."

"OK. So why?"

"Stroke. Never quite recovered. Didn't they give you her notes, a case history? Anyway I'm off. Take a chair from the kitchen if you want."

Mrs Agard spoke through her nose and the side of her mouth. She did not seem at all worried that a perfect stranger had come to sit with her.

"Mrs Agard I think there has been a mistake. I'm not from Social Services. I'm a journalist. I'm following up a story about your husband. Have the police talked to you?"

"Endlessly."

"About a missing person?"

"What else was there to talk about? He is missing."

"Have they spoken to you recently?"

"Not for a long time. Why? You don't look like police."

"I'm not. I said, I'm a journalist."

"Well, it makes no difference. I haven't seen him. What's it to you?"

"I think there's a story."

"A story? For the newspapers?"

"Yes."

"Ten years on, and you think there's a story?"

"A story waiting to be told."

"And what might that story be?"

"Too early to say."

"Or too late."

She paused, leant her stick against her knee, and slowly wiped her chin with a handkerchief.

"A story about a man who ran away, never to be seen again, perhaps. A man who for no reason abandoned his wife and two small children. Is that the kind of story you want to tell your readers? Is that your story?"

"It could be."

"You don't fool me."

"I'm not trying to fool you. I said, I don't know what the story will be yet."

"And how do you suppose I can help you?"

"I want you to think back... did your husband do or say anything unusual at about the time of the Druids Hill murders?"

"You think I can remember that far back? Remember clearly? We had a life together. Everything was normal: everything was significant, and at the same time, it wasn't. That's marriage."

"What do you mean?"

"Are you married? Have you ever been married?"

"No. but I've been close a couple of times. It's just never..."

"Then it is difficult to explain. My husband was a man of meticulous habits. His work demanded it. If he said he would be home by a certain time, then he was."

"Did he keep a diary?"

"A diary, no. He was not a very talkative man either, and I think he would have found keeping a diary a rather ridiculous idea. No, he kept a logbook. A different thing altogether. That was how he kept track of the computer work at the station."

"Mrs Agard do you know what happened to this logbook?"

"The police took it, I suppose. When he wasn't referring to it at home, planning work for the next day or the next week, he kept it at the station."

"And you still have no idea what happened to him?"

"To this day I have no idea, no clue, no reason."

"Did the police offer any compensation?"

"Why would they? There was no proof that his disappearance was work related so they didn't offer a penny."

"So you got?"

"Nothing... Absolutely not a penny, not from anyone. Really. I don't know. He just.... went. Everything was fine and normal, then suddenly he was gone. No warning. No word. No explanation. And since then, silence. He left me everything, all the bills, I got nothing but the bills. The girls got a trust fund. He set that up when they were born. At least they were provided for."

"Girls?"

"We had... have... two daughters. Then we were burgled.

What little we still possessed was damaged beyond repair. They trashed the place while we were at the solicitor's. And then I had a stroke. It was all too much for me, you see. We lost everything: car, TV, furniture. In all the fuss of the disappearance I had let the policies lapse, so we weren't covered. And then the life insurance wouldn't pay up on my husband either. No body, no crime, no case, no criminal, no conviction. As far as they were concerned, no death, you see."

"And where are your daughters now?"

"Left. Gone. As soon as they could get away. Neither of them wanted to be the last at home, in case they got lumbered with me. It was like a race to see who could get away first. Cool as you please. Must get it from their father. So how's your story looking now?"

"Dodgy, Mrs Agard. Very dodgy."

I wondered if the police would offer compensation now, if it was proved that Agard's disappearance had something to do with his work. And I wondered if Mrs Agard had kept up payments on her husband's insurance policy — just in case they ever found a body. I doubted it. But if she had, she'd be able to collect on the policy soon enough.

I left her there in the shadowed blue brick yard, wondering if I should have said they had found her husband's body.

Chronology: 1971

Fidel Castro visited Chile in 1971, and he made a speech at a very well attended public rally held in Santiago National Stadium. He said: 'A unique process is taking place in Chile. It is the process of change. It is a revolutionary process in which the revolutionaries are trying to carry out change peacefully by legal and constitutional methods, using the very laws established to maintain class domination. It is unique in the history of contemporary society. It is unique in the history of humanity.'

Jaime Perez-Cervera & Maria-Dolores Jamon
Augusto: The Little Book of the General

I gave Clifford a ring at the office. I had to hang on for ages.

"Hello?"

"Cliffie, darling, I want you to do something for me."

"If my wife hears you calling me Cliffie there's gonna be trouble, so just call me Clifford, OK?"

"OK, darling."

"And drop the darling bit as well."

"Clifford, sir."

"Emma…"

"All right. I'm just funning around. I want you to take a look at the station records, for me will you? Around the time of the Druids Hill murders."

"Can do, yeah. They're all down in the basement files. But what am I looking for?"

"I want you to see if you can find David Agard's station computer log book. He kept a record of all the work he did at the station: repairs, orders, installations that sort of thing. There might be several of these log books, but you're looking for the one covering the period from the murders at Druids Hill up to Agard's disappearance."

"A log book, right. Shouldn't be too difficult. What does it look like?"

"Like a log book. How should I know, I've never seen it."

"Yeah, OK. Then what?"

"No idea. Can you make a copy of it?"

"What? The whole bloody log?"

"Yes, Clifford, unless you can think of some other way of me getting to see it."

"Right. Might take a while, but yeah."

"Clifford, one last question… why has nobody told Mrs Agard that her husband has been found?"

"Dunno. Maybe they don't know where she is."

"My arse, Clifford. If I could find her, the police certainly could. It's not as if she's dodging about at high speed. In fact she's not moving about much at all, these days. Don't they have questions for her?"

"Well…"

44

"Exactly. You have a think about this Clifford... there must be a reason why no-one has told her. Oh and one last thing Clifford. You didn't tell me the name of the geezer in charge of the Druids Hill investigation."

"It was Chief Inspector Clough. Jarvis Clough. He retired early in the middle of the investigation. Dicky ticker. That's one of the reasons we never got a result. When he left, all the fizz went out of the investigation. He was the one who had all the information at his fingertips."

"Is he still alive? Where does he live."

"He had a place in Cheshire. Funny sort of a name. Juxta Frith. Something like that."

"Thanks Clifford, you're a brick."

"Eh, watch it."

Just as I arrived home a young chap in a dark suit wandered up to me. He was clutching an attaché case and a card folder and weaving a large bunch of keys. An Asian family followed him at a short distance.

"I hope you don't mind, but the owner has given permission for us to start showing the house to prospective buyers."

"Do I have a choice?"

"A choice. Not really. We were told you would not mind, but if it is a matter of considerable inconvenience to you..."

"And what did he tell you about me?"

"Just that you are flat-sitting for him."

"Which agency are you from?"

"Winstones, on the High Street."

"I see. Did the owner tell you I pay rent? That I'm a tenant? That I have rights guaranteed under law."

"What do you mean?"

"What I mean is that I have no intention of leaving. I'm a sitting tenant."

"But this is advertised as vacant possession."

"I know, but it isn't. I'm here and I'm staying."

"This is most embarrassing. Look, he specifically said

you were just looking after things for him, that you would move out."

"He's telling you porkies."

"Oh dear, this rather changes things."

"I think it does. Did you realise this place was up for sale with the Lewis's Agency until last week?"

"Yes, and the owner did mention that he found them rather dilatory, which was why he placed it with us."

"More porkies. Lewis's withdrew. They refused to act as agent when they realised he was not telling them the truth."

"But this means…"

"Yes, he's lied to you too. It also means that if you persist in showing this place to people under false pretences, you will be breaking the Trades Description Act."

"OK… I think we need to clarify matters… talk again with the owner."

"I think you do."

"What is going on here?" said the Asian man, stepping forward. "Can we see the house or not? Is there a problem?"

The clerk ushered the Asian family away from the house and began an explanation that was clearly excruciating.

It was a bit of a haul, but there was a direct train from Piccadilly Station right out to Juxta Frith. It was off the beaten track, miles from anywhere. It must have been a popular destination for the Manchester working class walkers and ramblers at one time. Not any more though. Now there were only two trains a day. Two trains there, and two trains back. Most people round these parts had cars. Large, expensive cars.

I found Jarvis Clough without any trouble, through directory inquiries. I'd rung him at once. I explained that I was a journalist looking to do a kind of famous mysteries from the past piece, and added that it was possible new evidence might be just about to surface. He was cagey, but intrigued. Even so, he'd agreed to meet me out at the Old Chapel on the edge of the golf course next day.

To call it a station is to dignify it mightily. In fact it was just a long platform with a single track. There was no station building of any sort — not even a ticket office. All around were the signs of recent demolition. The foundations of what had once been waiting rooms and offices poked up through the ground, and the remaining half of a pedestrian bridge now stepped off from the end of the platform with stairs to nowhere. The opposite platform had gone too. I wandered down the long ramp to the street. In a lay-by stood a solitary taxi.

"Do you know the Old Chapel?"

"On the golf course? Sure. Hop in."

"Any chance I could walk it?"

"Not unless you got all week."

"What happened to the station?"

"They blitzed it about two weeks ago, before anybody could organise a petition to save it. Listed building it was too. Beautiful hall with carved wood panels, bronze light fittings, lists of the fallen from the two world wars written up there in gold. Marble floors, lovely stained glass domed roof."

"But why?"

"Ask British Rail. They said it was too expensive to maintain."

"What a shame."

"Bunch of crooks. Sell their mum's false teeth, most of 'em. If they haven't done it already."

We drove across town and then out along a spur of woodland. We pulled up at a deserted spot. The driver pointed out the chapel in the distance. It was at the end of a long stretch of cinder track across the grass-covered dunes of the golf course. I was a couple of minutes early. The taxi driver said:

"This is as close as I can get. You'll have to walk the rest of the way. You want me to wait?"

"I might be a while… is there a bus?"

"Yeah… well there used to be a bus."

"OK. You'd better wait."

47

As soon as I got out of the car a stiff breeze battered my head, and sand stung my eyes. I crunched my way along the path out to the chapel. The wind pounded the trees and forced shock waves through the grass. I moved into the lee of the chapel and the wind dropped away. Out of the wind it was peaceful, with weak sunshine and nothing but the birds and the scudding clouds.

Off in the distance I could see a jogger in a purple and yellow track suit cresting the dunes of a bunker at a steady pace. I sat down with my back to the wall and waited. I don't know why but I expected Clough to arrive in a taxi too, so I kept an eye on the track. The jogger came over the last rise and headed straight towards me. He stopped, not even breathing heavily. A man in his late fifties with flecked iron grey hair.

"Well lassie, so what is it you want to know?"

"You're Chief Inspector Clough?"

"I was. Now I'm just Clough."

"Plain and simple."

"Plain maybe, but not so simple, I hope."

"Thought you had a bad heart."

"You thought wrong."

"I was misinformed."

"There's a lot of that about."

"Well let's try and set some things to rights."

"Is this for your story?"

"It is."

"Ask away. Lets go around to the sunny side of the chapel though. There's a bench."

We sat just out of the wind, looking out over the golf course, with a thin and watery sunlight bathing our faces.

"I'm beginning to cool down already."

"Is that bad?"

"Very bad."

"OK. So... has anybody else talked to you about the Druids Hill case recently?"

"Nobody has mentioned the case in, let me see... ten years."

"Tell me, were you likely to make an arrest on the Druids Hill job?"

"I thought so. We were definitely onto something."

"Why do you think that?"

"Well, we didn't get anywhere for a while. Then I came in to work one morning and there's people from MI6 — not Special Branch, mind, but Military Intelligence — in the ops room, on the computer, in my office, all over the bloody place. They wouldn't let us near anything. Then they called us all together in the duty room and collected our notebooks. And then I was called in to see the Chief Constable."

"God's right hand man."

"That's him. And this dick-head from MI6 points a finger at me and says: You are taking early retirement on full pension. I said: What about the case? He said: Stuff it matey, it's sorted."

"And that was it?"

"I was out of there less than ten minutes later. Didn't even get to clear my desk. Never went back."

"No explanation?"

"You're joking. Just a warning never, ever, to talk about this case."

"But you're talking to me."

"I'm not saying anything much. You probably know all this already, anyway. And what have I got to tell you? Bugger all really... so what's this new evidence that might surface?"

"Did you know Agard's body had been found?"

"Agard?"

"The station computer officer."

"Oh, Agard. I remember him..."

"They found his body a few days ago."

"And what has he to do with the case, d'you think?"

"I don't know. Something and nothing."

"Marriage problems I heard. After I'd gone though."

"Maybe. Maybe not."

"So, Agard's body you say. Tell me about it."

"It could be connected, but I'm not sure how."

"I'm listening."

"What?"

"Tell me what you know about the body, the circumstances."

"It was a shotgun to the chest. The same gun used at Druids Hill. Then he was dumped into the harbour at Dublin ferry port."

"Dublin? When exactly did Agard disappear?"

"Well, as far as I can make out he was off sick for a few days. Then his wife said he was missing."

"Hmm... that was just after I left."

"Was there a search for him?"

"All the usual I suppose. But I was out of it by then. Off the case. Off the force."

"So every effort was spared..."

"That is precisely what I suspect."

"And what do you suppose you had found at Druids Hill that brought about your retirement?"

"I've never been exactly sure. We had almost nothing to go on. No fingerprints. A trace on the shotgun, a tyre track, a single footprint. The car was from a hire firm at Luton airport. The assistant remembered two suntanned foreign men, possibly Spanish speakers. The gun was a pump action shotgun, made in the USA, not generally available here. The shoe print was from a trainer, not British."

"So you were thinking: Foreign."

"We were thinking: Foreign."

"Did you make any progress on the motive?"

"We were getting there. But slowly. Druids Hill had been rented out to Miller, the dead man, via an agency the previous year. Miller worked for the Non-Ferrous Metals Advisory Service. He collected statistics for the industry, organised business lunches, published brochures, yearbooks. That sort of stuff."

"And?"

"Well, it pans out like this, as far as we could see. Two

sun-tanned geezers, at least one of them speaking Spanish, wearing sneakers, arrive at Luton airport, hire a car, drive here. Either they smuggle the gun in with them or they pick it up somewhere along the way. They break into the farmhouse. Ransack the place, but don't find whatever it is they were looking for. Maybe Miller was there all the time. Maybe Miller comes home to find them waiting for him. Anyway they beat him, burn him. But they are disturbed by a kid delivering the newspapers. They kill the kid — maybe accidentally — but probably they would have had to kill him anyway because he'd seen them, seen what they were up to, seen something. Whatever he saw, it was too much. While they are dealing with the kid, Miller tries to make a break for it. They shoot him too. At this point they realise they've probably woken up the whole neighbourhood. Whatever it was they were looking for they are not going to find it now. And anyway, the job has suddenly got out of hand. So, they get in the car and drive off."

"So, we are looking for a pair of right callous bastards."

"Aye, but these are not just a couple of villains. Think. Two bodies, yes, but no fingerprints. Almost no forensic evidence. Nothing was stolen, though they had searched all the drawers in the place. These were professionals. Hired. Also they were armed. Your average villain doesn't go out to do a little thieving tooled up with a shotgun and a blow lamp. You had only to look at the state of Miller. A shotgun and a blowtorch for Christ's sake. Killers, yes. We had no motive, you see. We knew they were looking for something, something they thought Miller had, and they were prepared to torture, to kill, to get it, but that was all we knew."

"OK. So they were looking for something."

"Clearly."

"What?"

"Like I said, I haven't got a clue, sweetheart."

"Was anything taken from the house?"

"Not as far as far as we could tell."

51

"What about something from his work?"

"If they were after something Miller might have taken home from work, well, Miller's employers never noticed anything missing."

"So what could it have been?"

"If I knew that you would not be here."

"Drugs?"

"Probably not. Miller was absolutely clean. Though it could possibly have been drug money they were after. But my guess is they wanted information. Maybe documents. Anyway, that's about all I can tell you. I'm cooling down. I have to run some more or I'll get a chill. Let me know how you get on. If you have any more questions you know where to find me. And... if you should come up with anything I'd be glad to help."

"I appreciate the offer."

"You know, in my time I think I was a good copper. I mean I enjoyed my work, and I think I was fair. I caught my share of villains. But this case... it had no end to it. I was cut off. And I felt we were just about to get somewhere. I'm old fashioned, I know, but if I start something I like to finish it. I don't like being told by some wet fart that I've lost my job for no reason. It was *my* job. *My* case. I want to see it through. Whatever it is, I would like to be in on it."

"Even though they warned you off?"

"No. *Because* they warned me off."

"One last question?"

"OK, but make it quick."

"Where does Agard fit into this? Is he a red herring?"

"No idea, but I'll think on it. Keep in touch."

And with that Clough jogged off across the golf course, his purple and yellow track suit startling birds from the long grass.

The taxi was still waiting when I got back, but I had to find a cash point before I could pay him, and when I saw my balance I had more reason to worry. I thought, if this caper doesn't pay off big time before too long my landlord won't have to worry about chucking me out, I won't be able to pay the rent, I'll be living in a cardboard box.

It was late by the time I got home to my flat. I fed Beastly the cat and watched Maggie and Adolf swim in circles for a while. I even felt some sympathy with them until I remembered that they had a memory span of only about eight seconds, so they didn't actually know they were going round in circles. Although the man in the pet shop had assured me one was male and the other female, I had still not managed to find a way of telling which was which.

I had been keeping notes on the Druids Hill job, and now I set them out on the kitchen table, just to review what I had so far. I was hoping some kind of a story would emerge, something that I would be able to sell — an exclusive for one of the nationals, something that would get me a steady job again. But at about two o'clock in the morning I gave up, realised I had nothing but a collection of scraps and bits, nothing that made any sense, no story. Not yet, anyway. I went to bed.

I woke up to Beastly batting my face very gently with his paw. This is really his only gentle trick. When people ask me why he is called Beastly I always say 'Because he is Beastly'. Nobody believes me, of course. Until they try to stroke him. Then they understand. I took the hint from Beastly and got up quickly before he reverted to character. I gave him some food and put the kettle on. The doorbell rang, but whoever it was had gone by the time I got there. There was a parcel on the doormat. I opened it. The photocopied log. Good old Clifford. I made a pot of tea, cleared away my notes from last night and, still in my dressing gown, sat down to read. Two pots of tea later, still in my dressing gown, I had begun to get a grip on Agard's job at the police station.

Agard had two assistants, both civilian. The assistants trained all the coppers in how to access Criminal Records from the mainframe, how to cross check with Special Branch activities, contacting the Vehicle Licensing Centre in Swansea for car details, logging and updating crime reports, logging beat reports, notebooks and interview transcripts. And all this had to be done accurately, so that information could be cross-referenced for retrieval. The assistants also put ink ribbons and paper in the printers, ordered new equipment when things broke down, stood in for Agard when he had to attend conferences. Agard's main task was concerned with the system itself, with updating, developing and maintaining the programmes.

The log book was a tedious record of office life, a catalogue of non-events, a diary of what it took to run a station computer. There were no details of crimes, no dramas, only notes about repairs, maintenance records, issues of paper and ink ribbons — all signed and dated properly. There were notes on conferences attended, and training sessions, complaints from coppers who swore the machine could not spell. And there were the odd glitches — programme malfunctions, 'illegal acts', lost connections, downloads that never arrived, and even a system crash. I had to keep reminding myself this was all ten years ago, when computer technology was brand new and very clunky.

I reached the end of the log bleary-eyed and tired. Whatever it was I was looking for, I realised, it wasn't this. I rang Clifford at the office.

"Clifford."

"I thought I asked you not to ring me at work."

"Yeah well. I just wanted to ask you something. In the log I came across the letters UGHD. Do those letters — UGHD — mean anything to you?"

"Under Ground Hope Dispenser... Un-Godly Heap of Dross... Unloved Girls Hate Drama... It's from the log?"

"Yeah. According to Agard he did a UGHD just before Clough was sacked and just before Agard himself went missing."

"Great. Is it important? What does it mean?"

"That's what I'm asking. I know Agard did a UGHD, I just don't know what it is."

"And until you know what it is you…"

"Can't tell if it's important or not…"

"Well it's geek-speak, isn't it?"

"So I need a computer geek to translate for me?"

"Right."

"OK. Any press release on Agard yet?"

"No… all gone very quiet."

Harry the Hacker was my friendly local neighbourhood computer dealer. He had set me up with a nice little computer system a while back — nearly all of it legal — all at a massively reduced fee. Harry fancied me more than a little, I knew. But then he would, wouldn't he? Maybe I reminded Harry of his mum. I'm sure he had one. I liked Harry, but I did not fancy him, even a little bit. He was just a bit too ferrety for me. I think Harry realised this, but I don't think he minded that too much. He didn't hold a grudge, and he always seemed pleased to see me. The problem was that all Harry ever seemed to talk about was computers. He was an anorak. I'd never worked up the courage to tell him I had never used my machine for anything other than word processing. He would have been very disappointed, broken-hearted even. But then, I'd always wondered, just what do you do with a computer? Anyway, today I had what I thought was an intelligent question to ask him, so, mindful that I might not understand the answer I rang Harry and asked him out for coffee.

We meet in the spanking new Kangarouge Cafe, an Australian joint, part of the new development. Neutral territory. Neither of us had been there before. There were aboriginal dot paintings all round the walls, and didgeridoo music playing on the stereo. A waitress in a short black skirt and T-shirt wished us 'g'day' and handed us substantial menus. A chalk board informed us of the Specials: organic Ostrich burgers, organic Kangaroo Steaks. Another board listed Australian organic wines. All very South Manchester.

Harry looked pale, wormy in daylight. God help him, he was actually wearing an anorak. I ordered an espresso. Harry asked for instant coffee.

"The other stuff doesn't agree with me," he explained. He looked out of the window at the pub opposite. "I used to come here when I was a student. It was a good place to drink then. Used to go in there —" he gestured at the pub on the opposite side of the road. "It was a chrome-plated gin palace in those days, but the beer was cheap. And upstairs they used to have this geezer from the university teaching classes on science fiction. From the university!"

"Was he any good?"

"Very erudite. Really knew his stuff. But a bit of an academic nut, if you know what I mean. Anyway, round here used to be all right then. Now it's all tapas bars and organic kangaroo..."

"Harry what do the letters UGHD mean?"

"HD means Hard Disc. UG means Upgrade. Everybody knows that."

"Oh yeah... absolutely everybody, of course... I mean I knew that."

"So?"

"Well, yeah... That's what it means, OK... but what does it... mean?"

"It means that a computer hard disc is being replaced by a newer, faster, bigger, hard disc."

"Bigger?"

"Yeah. Look." Harry reached into his pocket. "This is a hard disc. You store data and programmes on here. It's only the size of a packet of cigarettes, but it can store gigabytes of information, thousands of pages of data. Incredibly economical, and getting better all the time."

"So they get... full. Right?"

"Eventually. Yes. They get full... eventually."

"And that's when you replace them?"

"Well, yes. But you replace them with a bigger, better disc, yes? In order to improve the speed or capacity."

"I see."

"And usually the larger the organisation the more discs they use, and the bigger the discs."

"So what size would, say, the police use in, say, an average city-centre nick, say?"

"Well depends when you're thinking of."

"Say, ten years ago."

"I see. That's very specific. Well all right, let's say ten years. Ten years ago. Early days. The chances are that an average sized city centre police station would have been about the same computer requirements as any small company, say a firm of accountants. Discs were very big then, and it wouldn't have been a high density job, like this one. It might have been one of a series, set up in a great big rotating plate rack, one on top of another, steel plates, all coated in black stuff."

"And how big would they have been?"

"For those days you would be talking at least a foot across, but it depends. It could have been as much as a yard across."

"That's big."

"Yes. But very advanced for those days."

"And how would you go about changing such a disc?"

"Well, nowadays it's quite simple."

"But in those days?"

"In those days it was a bit of a nightmare. First you had to transfer all the data onto tape. There's a special stuff called magtape. It looks like a can of film on a spool... anyway you transfer all the data onto one of these magtapes. Then, if it's one of these racks of plates you just twist and lift the whole thing out of the machine. Then you lower in the new hard disc upgrade, twist to lock it into place. Then all you gotta do is transfer all the material from the magtape back onto the new hard disc."

"And how long would all that take?"

"Well, like I say, those were early days. Putting in a new hard disc was easy. Transferring all the data would have been the real problem. It would have taken hours to get everything onto the magtape and then to take it all off again, to copy it onto the new hard disc."

"Would they do that at night?"

"Well, I don't know much about police procedures, but that would make sense. Most firms would do that kind of thing at night, when the office was shut or business was slack. The operator could take his time. You wouldn't want to be doing it while people needed to use the computer."

"Is it possible they would have stored data on floppy discs?"

"Possible, yes. Probable, no. You see, floppy discs in those days were big things about five inches across — and they really were floppy. But they weren't high density like the ones we use, so they didn't really hold that much data. To move stuff from a hard disc onto floppy discs — well you might need several hundred floppy discs, and it would take days. No, magtape was definitely quicker and more efficient."

I sipped my coffee, thinking about Agard's log book. UGHD. Simple. Was that all? A disc change? But another thought was forming. OK, so Agard had gone through the process of changing a disc. So what? According to his log book this was a fairly regular occurrence. So far, so good. And then I had my thought: but what was on the disc Agard changed?

I came out of my reverie to find Harry the Hacker starring at me across the table.

"Sorry... What?"

"I said, you didn't ask me out. For coffee. Did you, Emma? Not really you didn't..."

Chronology: 1971

The copper nationalisation laws were passed unanimously, with the co-operation of every political party, every senator and every deputy in the Chilean Congress. In addition the Chilean government also decided that years of extracting excessive profit from Chile, and failure to reinvest even a small percentage of that profit in Chile, had ruined the wealth of the Chilean state and the health of the Chilean population. As a result, no compensation would be paid to Kennecot, Anaconda or the other US companies for their mines. US Secretary of State William Rivers accused Allende of a serious departure from International Law and warned that the decision to nationalise the mines without compensation would have serious consequences.

Inevitably and almost immediately the Allende government came under severe pressure. The US cut economic aid to Chile from $159,000,000 to less than $15,900,000, and reduced loans from US banks by 95%. The US Export-Import Bank withdrew Chilean credit facilities worth $600,000,000. It has been estimated that at this time the CIA was spending over $8,800,000 on the Chilean black market [traded at 500% over the official rate, which is roughly equivalent to twenty times the total amount Richard Nixon spent on his 1968 election campaign]. They were using the black market to help drive up prices and ferment unrest among right-wing trades unionists, independent businessmen, civil servants and the military. By December 1971 taxis and buses could no longer find spare parts. Food shortages began to affect even middle class households. Protest demonstrations took place all over the country. These were followed by strikes in a whole range of industries and by the declaration of Martial Law in Santiago.

Jaime Perez-Cervera & Maria-Dolores Jamon
Augusto: The Little Book of the General

***

Mrs Agard had put on powder, rouge and lipstick. The effect in the late afternoon light of her gloomy backyard was rather ghastly, as if the ghost of her former self had come back to haunt her. She saw me looking.

"My dancing days are over. I do it to cheer myself up."

"Mrs Agard, you said you were burgled. When was that?"

"Yes. Right after David disappeared. They turned the whole place upside down."

"And what was taken?"

"Nothing."

"Nothing?"

"Not a thing. But they did a lot of damage. I thought because of the mess that it was just vandals, but the police said it was a very professional job."

"What did they mean by that? Thieves aren't usually what you might call amateurs."

"Well, the police know about these things. One of them said you could always tell if a place had been done over by a professional because when they open drawers, they start with the bottom one and leave them open. Then they don't have to waste time closing the drawers, but the open drawers don't get in the way as you move on to the next..."

"Very interesting."

"Well that's what he said. Maybe he was just making conversation."

"Maybe they were looking for something."

"Of course. But what?"

"How did your husband get on with his colleagues?"

"Colleagues?"

"The people he worked with."

"The police?"

"Yes."

"He got on well with his two assistants, the civilians. They came to dinner several times."

"And the police?"

"He tried. At first. But he was always uneasy with them. They only ever talked about bonuses, overtime, and he was sure a couple of them were taking bribes. There was a kind of syndicate. They sounded him out about joining, tried to draw him in, invited him to play golf, asked him to join the local lodge, but he wasn't interested. He stopped mixing with them. He wouldn't even eat in the canteen. Preferred to take sandwiches and a flask."

"Wasn't there anyone he got on well with?"

"Not among the coppers, no."

"What about Clough?"

"Clough was OK for a copper, I suppose. But David never felt right in his company either."

60

"Did he trust Clough?"

"I think, out of the whole bunch of them, Clough was the only one he did trust. He was on telly last year, did you see that?"

"What, Clough?"

"Yes, a follow up to the Miner's Strike. He comes from a small mining town, a village really, called Orgreave. You've probably never heard of it. During the Miner's Strike they used police horses there, used them like a cavalry charge to ride miners down in open fields. His mum and dad lived in Orgreave. They showed some film of the police cavalry charge and Clough was interviewed about the after effects. He said he couldn't go back there. Nobody, not even his own family, would speak to him. Nobody would speak to a copper. He said he thought Mrs Thatcher was turning the country into just what the communists said it was all along: class ridden, divided, repressive, violent. 'That's not policing,' he said. 'That's not what I trained for'. I watch a lot of television these days, but I remember it very clearly."

"Have the police been to see you?"

"Yes. They came this morning. Said they found David in Dublin harbour. Drowned, apparently."

"I'm so sorry Mrs Agard. Drowned? Did they say he drowned?"

"That's what I thought... it doesn't make sense."

"No. Why do you say that?"

"Well, drowned. I mean... David hated water. Had a real thing about rivers, lakes, harbours. Large bodies of water. He even preferred to take a shower rather than get into a bath. He would not go near water if he could avoid it. He couldn't swim. If he was drowned, if he was anywhere near water, it was not because he wanted to be, you can be sure."

It took a few days to track down the other members of Agard's computer team. One was dead in a drink-drive car crash. The other — Erno Trentino — had gone to work for

61

one of the multinational computer companies springing up in the Docklands development in the East End of London. The thought of forking out a wad of cash for a train ticket to London filled me with horror. But in the end, I thought, I've got no choice. Reluctantly I dug deep, bought a day return on the coach and set off for The Smoke wondering how I was going to get through to the end of the month, praying that some freelance work would turn up.

We met in Erno Trentino's office, in a brand spanking new glass cigarette box overlooking the river. Seems to me everything round that part of London looks onto the river. He sat back, flexed his embroidered braces and placed his hand stitched brogues on the desk while René, his highly manicured personal assistant, made us mocha-chino coffee. Erno polished his glasses and squinted at me. I opened up with: "So you gave up the police then?"

"You bet. First chance I got. Good experience, mind. But too many social problems."

"The people..."

"Exactly. Civilians always have a problem."

"And the money's better, I dare say."

"You dare say and a half."

He pointed out of the window to somewhere on the riverbank.

"You know, Charles Dickens used to go drinking in a boozer just over there... still there."

"What? That's taking the idea of after hours sups a bit far, don't you think?"

"No, not Dickens. The pub. The pub's still there."

"Ah, that's different."

"Incredible, eh?"

"Incredible."

"So you're doing a piece on David Agard. Funny business, that. Funny business altogether. You've met Mrs Agard? Always very nice to us, she was. A good cook, as I recall. And they've found his body in Dublin. I saw something about it in the paper. Maybe I should get in touch with her, you know, offer condolences. I wonder what he was doing there. And for all that time. So what's it to be, a kind of in depth profile of the man, or are you after the mystery angle? Don't tell me you think he was kidnapped by aliens."

"No, nothing like that. It's more a piece on missing persons in general. Are you still in the programming line?"

"No. I don't do any hands on stuff now. Haven't touched a keyboard in years. It's all development and management. Much more pleasant."

The coffee came. It was very good indeed. René withdrew his fingernails to the outer office closing the glass doors behind him.

"What can I tell you? David was always something of a mystery man. Not secretive, exactly. Definitely private. Did his job and went home to the family. The police didn't like him much. They reckoned he had a poker up his arse. But they couldn't fault his work."

"Was there a scam?"

"Probably. But David wasn't part of it. The rumour was that the Serious Crimes Squad spent more time collecting bribes and protection than they ever did investigating. I mean, their record was a disaster: no wonder they were disbanded. The only surprise is that it took so long. We had to process all their time-sheets, reports, expenses and everything onto disc. It was fairly obvious they were up to something, but you could never get a handle on it, never say exactly what. You know, you could look at a document and say there's something funny here, but what exactly? And anyway, that was not our line of business. We didn't do investigations. We were just computer support."

"Do you think any of this had a bearing on David's disappearance?"

"I just don't know. One minute he was there. The next he wasn't. That's disappearing for you."

"What was going on around the station at that time, the Druids Hill inquiry?"

"All the usual stuff. We'd been pretty busy with the Druids Hill job. We'd been told to set up an information

63

retrieval system, so that we could pick up references to people across a whole series of reports by cross indexing. Now it would be a piece of cake, but then we were making it up as we went along. And then one morning we came in to work and we were told there had been a system crash overnight. They had called in a specialist to sort it. And there was someone in the computer room. He was finishing just as we arrived, but we had to wait in the corridor until he left. And this was very odd because, when there was a problem — even a serious problem like a system crash — they wouldn't let anyone but us sort it out. That was our job. They would even phone us at home, send a car for us. We were the authorised personnel, you see. Anyway I remember the man very clearly. Although he was dressed in civvies he was military, I'm sure. Something about his style, the suntan, the crew-cut, the white teeth — all porcelain, I think. His body language was... focused. He didn't look at anybody, didn't speak. He carried a briefcase under his arm instead of gripping it by the handle and he... well, he walked like an American."

"What do you mean?"

"I don't know exactly. Difficult to describe. He wasn't just walking down the corridor. It was like he was conscious of the fact that he was *walking*. Taking up space, covering ground, moving like he had a purpose. I can't describe it, but you'd know it if you saw it."

"But this is ten years ago."

"True, but still clear in my mind."

"What did you make of all this?"

"Well what could we make of it? David and I had worked late the previous night and there had been no sign of any problem. And if there had been a problem it should have been David they called in, not some outsider."

"Why had you worked late?"

"It was a regular slot. Once a month or so, David liked to run a systems check. And when necessary he upgraded the hard disc."

"And he had done this the previous night?"

64

"That's right. I'd stayed on to help. We took it in turns. Lifting the old disc out and lifting the new disc in. It was tricky. Needed four hands. It was a long job in those days too. Now you can do it in a couple of minutes, but then it involved copying everything onto magtape, changing the disc and then copying the magtape back onto the disc. And that's what we did. I don't reckon we could have finished much before about two, maybe three, in the morning. Next morning, when they let us back into the computer room, David asked what the problem had been. All they said was not to worry, all fixed now. So David and I immediately ran another series of checks. But we couldn't find anything wrong, and no trace of a problem. And then, I remember, David said: This is not the disc I put in last night."

"What?"

"Well, they had replaced the disc that David had just replaced."

"Replaced it?"

"Yes."

"But why?"

"We had absolutely no idea. A complete mystery."

"And then what happened?"

"Well, next day we were all told that Inspector Clough had had a heart attack, stress, and was taking early retirement. At the end of the week we were told there was little chance of an arrest so they were going to ease off on the investigation. The following day David called in sick. That was the last we saw of him."

"And the investigation gradually just collapsed."

"Not even gradually. I mean it just stopped."

"OK... so let me see if I've got this straight. You and David stayed late, copied the station hard disc with all the Druids Hill files onto a new disc. And that night the new disc was itself replaced with another new disc by someone else — possibly an American military type."

"Right, yeah."

"So presumably the Yank didn't know Agard had just

completed an upgrade."

"Because Agard had not had time to tell anyone or to enter it into the log book."

"And presumably the Yank took away what he thought was the old disc."

"Probably. Possibly."

"You didn't notice that?"

"No. I can't say I did."

"But you remember he was carrying a brief case?"

"Right."

"And the disc could not have been in there?"

"No. The disc was much too bulky."

"OK. But the disc the Yank put in is probably now in the station archive?"

"Dunno. But, yes, I would think so. Very probably, yes."

"So what I want to know is..."

"Where is the disc David took out?"

"Precisely. That would be in the station archive too... Wouldn't it?"

"In theory, yes, but it was late when we finished."

"Yes."

"So, perhaps David didn't want the trouble of securing the old disc in the basement."

"Ah. So what if he simply put it in the boot of his car, say? What if he took it home with him, intending to put it into the station archive next morning?"

"Only, next morning..."

"Only, next morning, when you arrived the American was there and you were locked out."

"Right."

"So maybe he smelled a rat. Maybe he didn't put the old disc in the archive after all."

"But he was very methodical."

"Is there any chance I could get to see the disc?"

"Fat chance. It was kept in a strong room, an armoured vault, under the station. That was ten years ago, but I don't suppose it's much different now. You'd have to get permission from the Home Office, and even then you'd probably have to get a Court Order. And by the time you did all that..."

"The disc would have been mysteriously disappeared. Or wiped."

"But you know there is an easier way."

"There is?"

"There is. I'm fairly certain David put the old disc into the archive. I mean, even late at night that's what he would do. And if he had taken it home with him that night, which is unlikely, next day, even with the upset about 'the problem' and the American, he would have found time to do it. That's how he was."

"So?"

"So by concentrating on the disc you give yourself a headache."

"I do?"

"Yes, don't worry about the disc. Ask yourself, where is the magtape copy?"

"I've heard about magtape..."

"The magtape copy of the disc. We transferred everything from the original disc onto magtape, then changed the disc and transferred everything from the magtape onto the new disc."

"So... what you're saying is: what happened to the magtape?"

"Precisely. Fact is, everybody was all worked up about security for the discs — Home Office Regulations — but nobody gave a toss about the magtapes. They just slung the old magtapes in a steel cupboard in the basement corridor and left them."

"So you reckon David would have put the disc away safely that night, as per regulations, but you also reckon he'd probably have just put the magtape in the cupboard."

"Right."

"So if I could access the magtape I'd know what was on the original disc... the one the Yank took away."

"Absolutely. If you could find it."

"If I could find it."

"And if you could read it."

"If I could read it?"

"Yes. You have to find a way to read it."

"Read the magtape. And is that difficult?"

"Bloody difficult."

"I should have guessed."

"It's not impossible."

"Just difficult."

"Very."

"One last question. What was Clough like as a copper? Did you trust him?"

"Yeah, I think you could trust him. He'd been a copper for a long time, came up from beat bobby, through the ranks, as it were. He knew his patch. Old style police. And he loved his work. He was respected — not feared, mind. Respected. Neighbours, people in the area talked to him. He knew most of the villains by name. And he knew their mums and dads and cousins too. But he used to say: 'Crime changed. Criminals changed. The police changed. The world changed.' He always had a lot of questions for the young coppers just starting — questions police life does not encourage you to pursue. I remember, one time, in the locker room, some rookie was mouthing off about getting CS gas, and Clough listened for a while, then he said: 'What is the difference between the communist regimes — the police state and all that — and what we're doing here?'"

"And the answer?"

He waited but nobody said a word. And then he said: 'Maybe, it's a question of degree... keep people in their place: pay rises for coppers, unemployment for everyone else. Most people think policing is outside politics. But it isn't, it never was.' Clough knew that, you see."

I got back from London very late that night. My flat felt cold, strange, empty. There was a funny smell. I thought maybe the drains are on the blink — that's all I need. Maybe I was just getting paranoid, but the smell bothered me. I felt uneasy, as if there was someone in the flat. I took a hammer from the toolbox under the sink and cautiously checked each room. I even checked under the bed. Nothing. This Druids Hill job was making me jumpy. I fed Margaret and Adolf — the one I thought was the female beat the other to the food. Typical, I thought. And even if I'd got them the wrong way round and it was the male who got to the food first, I could still smirk and say: Typical. I put a pot of tea on the table — my own mixture of red label and Earl Grey, a special treat for times of stress — very tasty, very refreshing. Then I put a notepad and pencil nearby. I laid a towel across my lap. Beastly was waiting for this. It was our agreed sign that he could jump onto my lap. He's not allowed up without the towel, or I get cat-hairs all over me. He's not normally affectionate, but tonight he kept turning about as if he could not get comfortable. And even when he stopped turning and settled down, he stayed wide awake, which is most unlike him. I thought vaguely that he had probably had a fight with another cat, but he did not appear to be damaged.

I took up the pencil and began to draw diagrams. Whichever way I drew things, Agard's disappearance was linked to the computer disc. The possibility of an American mixed up in all this was puzzling, but I had to hold back on that, just in case it was a red herring. It was no good, by the third cup of tea I had to admit that nothing hung together. Too many missing pieces, bits. No thread from which to make a story. I could not find a way to link the problems of the local nick with the Druids Hill murders, and could not find a connection to the discovery of Agard's body. Not yet, anyway.

I turned on the radio in time for the news. There was a brief item about Agard's body being found, drowned, but no mention of his connection to the Druids Hill case and no mention of any shotgun wound. I wondered if Clifford could have got it wrong about the shotgun. And then I started to wonder — got it wrong? Maybe he lied. But why would he do that? He had told me what he knew as soon as he heard. If that was not what the police were saying now, officially, on the news, that was not Clfford's fault. Also, the more I thought about it, the more I came to think that Clifford's decision to put me onto this story in the first place was more than a bit mysterious. Suddenly cold tea seemed inappropriate. I reached for the bottle of gin from behind the toolbox under the sink.

Chronology: 4 March-11 September 1973

Half of the Senate and the entire Chamber of Deputies were due to run for election that year. Political pundits forecast a heavy defeat for Allende, but the Chilean people, in spite of the hardships they were suffering, still supported Allende's reform programme. Overall, Allende's Popular Unity Party gained 43.4% of the vote, increasing the Party's seats in Congress by eight. However, at the end of June discontented troops surrounded the Presidential Palace. Only after several hours of fierce fighting in which 22 people were killed, were the rebels subdued. Allende felt he had no option but to seek a mandate to continue. He did this by calling a national referendum to judge his economic policies. The referendum was to be held on 11 September 1973.

The night before the election, however, the Chilean Navy, which was supposed to be taking part in joint manoeuvres with the US Navy out in the Pacific, suddenly returned to port and immediately sent shore parties to round up Allende's supporters. A US guided missile cruiser, two destroyers and a submarine anchored just outside Chilean territorial waters. In the early hours of the morning General Augusto Pinochet staged a military coup. Allende, who had got wind of the coup, placed himself with troops defending the Presidential Palace and addressed the nation on the radio. The Palace, surrounded by tanks and hundreds of Pinochet's soldiers, was bombed from the air. The Palace defences were finally penetrated by commandos. It was said Allende was killed during the fighting by a burst of machine gun fire. However, there are several photographs of Allende in existence, taken after the fighting had finished. It seems more likely that he was captured and then executed.

Jaime Perez-Cervera & Maria-Dolores Jamon
Augusto: The Little Book of the General

Two days later I got a letter from my landlord. It was a rant. He refused to pay any repair bill for my kitchen wall, and threatened me with eviction if I started any repairs without permission. He wrote: 'How dare you interfere with my Estate Agent. I have instructed them to sell my house. And you have prevented this. Your action is a calculated move to arrogate the powers of a legitimate owner to yourself.'

I sat down at once to write a reply. 'Dear Sir, I am not calculating a move to Harrogate. But I would like you to fix my wall...'

Then I noticed the postmark and stamp on his letter. Singapore. My wit would be wasted at that range. I thought I'll just pop round to my solicitor, show him the letter and see what he has to say. And on the way I'll take my washing to the laundrette. I scattered a pinch of food for the fish, put out a plate of cat biscuits for Beastly — he hissed his thanks — packed a bag of smalls, put the landlord's letter in my pocket and set out, only to find Clifford sitting in a car directly outside my front gate.

"This your car, Clifford?"

"This is my car."

"You sure? It looks like a company car to me. Very upmarket."

"Look at the number plate."

I looked at the number plate.

"CU2?"

"Personalised plates."

"CU2 — See You Too?"

"Clifford Usher. Get it? Annette, my wife, thought of that."

"Nice one Annette.... Very clever. But why 2? Was your dad Clifford Usher the First? Or have you got two cars?"

"Nah, that's 'cause the kids on the street kept adding 'nt' in indelible ink. Now they don't have the space for it."

"But it's a professional joke too, right."

"Eh?"

"I mean, you're a copper, yeah?"

"Yeah. So?"

"Didn't you do science at school?"

"Dunno what we did at school. What's that got to do with anything?"

"CU2. The chemical symbol for copper."

"Copper?"

"Yeah. This is a copper's car. The number plate says so."

"Christ. That's like a bloody advertisement...."

"Clever girl, your Annette."

"Yeah. Very clever. I can see I shall have to have a word with her about chemistry and that. Look, Emma I'm in a rush. I found the stuff you wanted."

"So the disc is there."

"Discs."

"Discs? Plural?"

"If that means more than one, yeah. It's a set."

"That's right. And it's a kind of big thing?"

"Yes. It's a kind of big thing."

"I see. And how big is the thing?"

"The whole contraption is about eighteen inches deep. A series of metal plates about an inch thick, the size of a very large dinner plate across, and they're all inside a kind of rack with a thick plastic cover, like a budgie's cage."

"OK. Well done Clifford. That's great."

"Well what do you want me to do now?"

"I'm not sure, but I might ask you to get hold of the discs for me."

"Not a chance, sister. Not a chance. I couldn't get them out of the building."

"You sure?"

"I'm positive."

"Damn. We'll just have to wait until the right moment. Anything new on Agard."

"Yeah, there's been some stuff on the news and there's something — a press conference — planned for tomorrow."

"Sluggish. Very sluggish."

"Listen Emma... I'm going to have to ease off a bit for a

while."

"What do you mean?"

"I mean I can't be seen with you. I won't be able to help you. Nothing serious, but you'll have to get by without me for a bit."

"Clifford, you started this."

"Yeah, and now I'm asking you…"

"What? Why?"

"I didn't realise. I thought it would just be a story for you… get you back into the swim, you know…"

"But?"

"I didn't realise it would turn into this."

"This?"

"Yeah."

"This what? Turn into what?"

"There's more to it than I thought. What you're asking me to do. I can see where it's going… you're pointing the finger at the police."

"Shotguns and blowtorches? Doesn't sound like local plod to me."

"Maybe not, but they are involved in this somehow, that's why you're after the discs. And that puts me in a very awkward position. I work with these people."

"OK. But you weren't in on it, whatever it was."

"So bloody what? I'm a copper."

"You help me with this Clifford, and if I come up with something, I'll hand it straight to you. I promise. You'll come up whiter than white. Sorry. Bad choice of phrase. But you take my point?"

"I take your point. It's just… I'm very visible. This is my career. I'm a sergeant. I'm black and that makes a difference. I've waited and worked. I can't throw it away."

"OK. I do understand, Clifford. Honest. But before I leave you alone I need a copy of the coroner's report on Druids Hill. Not the delivery boy just the man, Miller, plus any forensic follow-up."

"What? Didn't you hear what I just said?"

"I heard you Clifford and I'm prepared to overlook it

73

just this once."

"Emma for Christ's sake."

"I need this stuff Clifford, then I'll leave you alone OK?"

"Are you onto something?"

"Maybe. Probably not. Do I get the stuff?"

"Depends."

"On what Clifford dear?"

"I get you this, and then I'm out of it. Permanently."

"Permanently? And what does that mean? For a long while?"

"No, it means for good."

"Well, if that's what you want."

"It's what I want."

I got out of the car and Clifford drove off. I sat in the launderette for a few minutes thinking about this conversation. I should have predicted it, I suppose. But then I laughed. There's a part of Clifford that likes to bully and there's a part that likes to be bullied. But I had to admit, there had been an edge to his voice. He wasn't playing around. He was serious. If anything, I'd say he was scared. Yes. Definitely scared. Anyway, after a couple of minutes watching my stuff go round in sudsy circles, I popped round to the solicitor to show him my landlord's letter.

True to his word, three days later Clifford dropped the copies of the forensic and coroner's reports on Miller through my letter box. A plain buff envelope containing a cardboard file of photocopied pages. I sat down to read it immediately. The coroner's report was grim: a catalogue of burns, bruises, rope marks and shotgun damage. There was precious little there for me. The forensic report was totally uninteresting except for one line which caught my eye. A sentence that read: 'Under the finger nails of both hands deposits of sand and cement, in the hair traces of wallpaper paste'. It looked as if Miller had been doing a spot of DIY just before he died. DIY? What sort of DIY would that be? Miller did not sound like the kind of man who was interested in home improvement. I thought it's time I went and had a look at the house.

Chronology: September 1973

General Pinochet declared a state of war. He promoted himself to the position of President and brought in CIA 'advisers'. Over the next 15 years, in a systematic campaign to destroy the left wing, thousands of trade unionists, oppositionists, Socialist Party members and others considered sympathetic to socialism were arrested and detained. In total perhaps as many as 200,000 people were arrested and tortured by electric shock, beating, animal rape and solitary confinement for periods up to a year. In Santiago the 8,500 seat Chile Stadium and the 80,000 seat National Stadium became torture and execution centres, holding thousands of prisoners for months at a time.

Several hundred people were tried and executed by military tribunals. Others were imprisoned in the Atacama Desert, on ships off Valparaiso, around Punta Arenas, or on the frozen Dawson Island. Some simply 'disappeared', their headless corpses dumped in the Nuble river or into the sea off Talcahuano. In total an estimated 5,000 people died at the hands of the Pinochet regime. In August 1987 General Pinochet explained: 'Every so often, democracy has to be bathed in blood.'

Jaime Perez-Cervera & Maria-Dolores Jamon
Augusto: The Little Book of the General

I was up before dawn, feeling slightly better since the solicitor had told me that as my landlord was clearly trying to sell the house without acknowledging that I was a legitimate tenant, the estate agent would probably withdraw from acting for him, lest they get done under the Trades Descriptions Act. As far as my solicitor could see, unless my landlord came up with something very underhand, he was stymied.

I packed a rucksack for the day, sandwiches, thermos, a local guidebook, a torch, few other bits and bobs, and set off for the house at Druids Hill. I was not sure what I was looking for, and not sure how long it would take me to find it. But I certainly wanted to be there before the locals were up and about.

I'd been over to Druids Hill several times in the past to cover local interest stories. The house was located on a hill, right next to an old geological fault line, so although on one side the road wound along country lanes across gently rolling countryside, on the other side the land dropped away sharply in a forty foot cliff, known as The Littel Edge. My guide book, borrowed from Didsbury library more than a decade ago and never returned, said Druids Hill (the Victorian cartographer had not been tempted to add an apostrophe), just back from The Edge, had once been an important Celtic site. In the field at the back of the house, just before The Edge dropped away, there was a circle of standing stones dating back to pre-historic times. It was supposed to have been a site of Druid ceremonies at the time of the Celts. But the Romans had sorted the Celts out, good and proper. They always did. They slaughtered all the Druids, then built a small fort with earth walls and a wooden palisade. But that had been abandoned almost before it was completed, long before the Legions were called back to Rome. There was talk of buried treasure — Roman or Druid. But the most anyone had ever found was a lot of broken pottery, some decayed leather the experts claimed were Roman sandals, and a set of carved bone dice. Once in a while — for midsummer, equinoxes, eclipses, that sort of thing — modern Druids assembled there. I had covered several of their meetings. Old madmen in long white numbers — always a good photo opportunity, my editor used to say. Good for at least half a page.

And once in a while The Golden Clasp Society, a Civil War re-enactment group, would put on a show. In the seventeenth century King Charles I had stayed there one night, fleeing defeat in the Civil War. His personal bodyguard of gentlemen made a desperate last ditch effort among the standing stones, but were finally chased over The Edge to die on the stones below. Typical, I thought.

The big cheese gets off, but his minions get slaughtered. Somehow it had always been a bit of a jolt to see pretend Cavaliers and Roundheads blasting away at each other with flintlock pistols among the great standing stones. I'd covered several of their shows too, over the years.

It was still dark when I got off the local train from Piccadilly. There was a heavy frost. Very pretty, but it made my teeth chatter. And there was a thick mist rolling in from the west, off the Irish Sea. I walked out of town and along the foot of The Edge till I reached The Rake, a steep heavily wooded lane that cut up through The Edge. I was panting by the time I reached the top and moved slowly to find the turn off that led through a birch copse, towards the house.

The birch trunks glimmered in the early light. A JCB digger turned in off The Rake behind me. It forced me to push back into the hedgerow as it passed. The driver waved cheerily and headed between the overhanging trees towards the house at the top of The Edge. I followed the digger up the lane, and then stood to one side among the bushes, to get a look at the house. The dawn was coming up behind the house, so I could really only see it in silhouette. A lorry bounced up the lane smacking branches aside and came to a groaning halt. Three burley navvies in donkey jackets jumped down. A large brown Jag pulled up behind them. A man in a long coat and gloves got out — clearly the boss. He spoke briefly with the men, then got back into the car and drove off. The navvies set about loading wood and coal into a brazier. They were building a fire. I had not expected this. I don't know what I had expected. I just know I had not expected this. And I kept cudgelling my brain, saying: Come on Emma, think of something to get you in there. Think! Think fast!

I sidled over to the man I took to be the foreman and wished him a good morning. He did not seem at all surprised that I was there.

"So what's the plan then, chief?" I said.

"We're tearing it down," he replied. "Levelling the whole shebang."

"Why's that?"

"It's standing idle. Been empty for years. Nobody will take it on. Haunted maybe, after the murder. You know about that?"

"Yes, I remember."

"Anyway a farmer over the way there has bought the land and he's planning to build a pigpen on the site."

"Let's hope pigs don't mind ghosts."

"He could have problems."

"What d'you mean?"

"Why, now, people don't realise, but pigs are very sensitive animals."

"Is that fact?"

"The pig is a much maligned animal."

We walked the long curving drive, between dark rhododendron bushes and roses that had gone wild. Framed by the trees the house was an impressive gothic job with arched windows, wide, black double front doors, and loads of stained glass.

"It's a great shame, a big house like that going to waste."

"It's a listed building, you know? Classic Victorian with typical domestic features. It's mentioned in the local guide books."

"Sure I know that, Missy."

"And you still want to knock it down."

"I don't want to do any such thing. It's a grand old place. But listed or not I have instructions to demolish it, and unless someone comes through here with a court order to stop me I'm going to do just that."

"I used to live there when I was a little girl," I said, lying fluently.

"Did you now? Really? Is that how come you know so much about it?"

"Yeah."

"Well, you're back just in time. If you'd come next week

78

it would just be a hole in the ground."

"It has memories for me."

"Of course, it would... it would."

"My father... well never mind. Let's just say..."

"Memories."

"Memories."

"Would you like to take a few minutes?" He gestured at the house.

"You wouldn't mind?"

"Not at all."

"Is it safe?"

"Safe as houses. Structure is still sound. There's a few rotten floor boards, but I was in there myself a couple of days ago."

"When do you start work?"

"We have the services and the outhouses to take care of first, before we really get started. And anyway, we won't move until after we've had a spot of breakfast. Take as long as you like."

"Thanks. I really appreciate this."

The house was dark, cold, damp, crumbling. Light filtered weakly through the filthy stained glass fanlight above the door. About halfway along the wide passage the wall was gouged and scored with slashes and pits from a shotgun blast. This, I knew, was where they had found the body of the newspaper boy. In the scullery beyond the kitchen area there were more marks on the wall. On the flagstone floor it was just possible to make out faint chalk lines that had once marked the spot where Miller's body had been found.

All very interesting I thought, but not what I came for. But then, I did not know exactly what I was looking for. All I knew was that I would recognise it as soon as I saw it. Whatever it was. I moved carefully, slowly from room to room, floorboards creaking, dust drifting and sifting. I pushed my way through a curtain of cobwebs and climbed the stairs, clutching the great carved wooden banister. There were two bedrooms on the first floor, two box rooms and a bathroom. From the first floor landing a narrow staircase led up to what must at one time have been the servant's quarters on the top floor. I manoeuvred carefully through more cobwebs and went up.

I pushed open the door to find myself in an attic room with a low sloping ceiling. I looked out from the attic window. Down below the demolition crew had a small brazier set up and a flame was just beginning to lick over the top. They were just about to start cooking breakfast. I wondered if they would cook bacon and eggs on a shovel. Isn't that what navvies are supposed to do? Off to one side I could just make out the line of The Rake as it topped the brow of The Edge. To the other I could see over the trees to the field at the back of the house where the stone circle glimmered white in the dawn murk. I turned back to the room and there on the opposite wall, where the weak light slanted across the chimney breast, was what I was looking for. A patch of wallpaper, the same colour and design as the rest of the wallpaper, but slapped on in haste with the swirling floral pattern running from left to right instead of top to bottom.

I set down my rucksack, took out a lump hammer and a chisel and set to work. Half an hour later I was covered in brick dust, but I had what I wanted. Erno Trentino had been wrong. Agard had not put the discs in the station strong room. The discs that Clifford had found were the ones the mysterious Yank had substituted. The original discs, the ones Agard had removed the previous night, were here in the wall.

I could hear the workmen in the hall downstairs. I stuffed my prize into the rucksack and made my way back through the lace curtain of cobwebs. The workmen were busy stripping lead pipe from the old outhouses. I don't think they saw me leave.

"Harry I need a favour."

"Yeah? Like before?"

"Not exactly."

"I'm still smarting from the last time. The fact you

wanted me for my mind rather than my body. How is a feller to cope with the modern woman? I mean ter say."

"I apologise, Harry, but there's a time and a place for everything."

"And the time and place was?"

I could sense this was a reproach. I had not responded to Harry the way he would have liked.

"Never mind all that for the moment Harry, we'll get to it eventually."

"Promise?"

"I promise." Now I was flirting a little.

"Yeah, yeah, sure you do." He did not sound convinced.

"I promise. I do."

"Yes you are very promising… however?"

"Yes. However."

"Like I thought."

"Trust me, Harry. The time will come."

"Just like Christmas."

"Well this time there's a bottle of 43 year old Highland malt in it."

"Ah, well, that's different."

"You mean bribery works?"

"No. Just business is business."

"Since when am I business, Harry?"

"Since you invited me out for coffee just to pick my brains. Now…"

Harry's flat was exactly the sort of place you would expect an anorak to have. There was a wall full of well-thumbed science fiction paperbacks, a sink full of dishes, several months' dust on everything and rooms full of computer equipment so complex that it made NASA look like a square wheel. Typical boy's stuff, I thought. Most of the flat had not been decorated since before Harry moved in — at a guess I'd have put that sometime at the end of the 1960s. Not that Harry noticed. But the sitting room was the exception. It had been repainted recently leaving the walls a startling yellow.

"Harry, did your decorator wear dark glasses by any chance?"

"Cor, you are a bit of a detective, aren't you? Yeah, he used to get really bad migraines from time to time. How did you know that?"

"Oh, just a wild guess Harry."

"The trained observant eye of the professional journalist, eh?"

"What's all this then?" I said, pointing at the wall.

"That's my crossbow," said Harry proudly.

"I know what it is Harry, I'm just a little surprised..."

"I practice regular. I'm in a club. Have been for years. We do longbow mostly." From under the settee he pulled a longbow and quiver of arrows. "And every year we invite the press, get all dressed up and do a kind of mini re-enactment of Agincourt."

"Did you ever do anything with the Golden Clasp Society? I used to cover their re-enactments up at Druids Hill."

"That bunch of wankers — if you'll pardon my French. No chance."

"You don't like them?"

"Why should I? All they do is ponce about with fake muskets, pretending. We actually get out at weekends and practice a skill."

"A skill?"

"Yeah. Archery. The longbow was the Ouzi machine gun of its day; all fine and historical, but it needs to be practised. But even so, one on its own isn't very accurate, you know?"

"Unless you're Robin Hood, of course."

"Very funny. Now the crossbow, that's a different matter. Very accurate at short range. A crossbow bolt will go right through chain mail, even some of the modern Teflon body armour, too."

"So you're more of a William Tell than a Robin Hood."

Harry did not look amused.

"So what's this favour, and where's my malt?"

I hauled the cake rack of computer discs out of my bag and handed it to Harry. He set the drum down on the table and carefully, almost reverentially, wiped away the film of brick dust. It was a transparent plastic case about the width of a dinner plate across, over a foot deep, with a metal lid and handle. Inside you could see perhaps a dozen thin discs, all matt black.

"Strewth. I ain't seen one of these outside a museum. Actually, come to think of it, I ain't even seen one in a museum. Now let me guess. You want me to access this for you."

"That's the general idea."

"Could take a while. Technology moves on, you know. Programmes these days are much more sophisticated. I might have to write a special programme. Be like trying to read hieroglyphics."

"Any danger of a cup of tea, Harry?"

"Not much, unless you make it yourself."

Harry had already set to work.

I cleared a space in the sink, boiled some water, washed two of the less unacceptably stained mugs and then raided the cupboards to make us both a cup of something hot and strong. Well that was the intention, but in the end it had to be instant decaf with powdered milk and saccharine pills. Harry drank it without a word. I turned archaeologist to dig through layers of electronics magazines to rediscover the sofa, stretched out and pulled my coat over me.

"Harry, have they invented central heating on your planet?"

"Expected any day now."

At about six in the morning Harry shook me awake.

"What is it Harry, you found the chocolate biscuits?"

"You never answered my question. Where's my malt?"

Gummy-eyed I reached into my bag and brought out a bottle of malt whisky. Harry took it.

"You lied. Says here it's 42 years old."

"So?"

"You said 43 year old."

"I bought it last year."

Harry punched a couple of buttons and a page swam into view with lists of files and directories.

"This is as far as I can get, I'm afraid. But you ain't getting the whisky back 'cause I've spent all night on this."

"But this is brilliant."

"No, it ain't. It's a start though. Normally you could open up any of these files from this page. There's tons of stuff. But my programme — superior though it is — will only read the directory. It won't open the files. I've tried it every possible way. The thing is, we moved on."

"Eh?"

"Well the stuff on this carousel is more than ten years old. In computer terms that's ancient. Several computer generations. At least three, maybe five or six."

"So?"

"Well, you're asking me to step back into the past. Programmes grow and develop over time. While the next one can probably read the last one, the one after that will have difficulty. And by the time you get to the programme after that, it will be impossible. It's a bit like asking Einstein to repair a TV set, or getting an astronaut to fix a valve radio. None of the programmes I can run will open or display a programme more than a couple of years old. Beyond that and it's just too primitive for modern computer programmes to read. Like I say, things have moved on."

"Can you think of any way we can get into it?"

"Well, if you can find a copy of the original programme, I could load it, probably. And maybe then we could read the stuff."

"How likely is that?"

"On a scale of one to ten, about minus three. Nobody keeps old programmes. Especially programmes tailored for people like the police or the military."

"Any more bright ideas?"

"Well if this disc was upgraded, there's probably a magtape copy somewhere."

"Magtape... yeah. Well, at least I know what it is. And you could read that?"

"No, I couldn't."

"Great."

"But I know someone who could."

"A pal?"

"A pal of sorts, yes."

"OK. Harry, do you think you can give this pal a call."

"I could but..." Harry clutched the whisky bottle to his chest.

"But what Harry? What? You want a date? All right, we'll fix a time and go out for dinner... a drink. Whatever you like... just phone... please..."

"No, that's not it."

"What, Harry? What do you want?"

"I want to know what's going on. What are you up to?"

"Why? You don't need to know."

"Are you kidding? You've got me trying to read police files — these are police files, aren't they? Even from ten years ago, this is illegal. Whatever you're up to is deeply dodgy. I need to know exactly what it is before I go any further."

"It's safer that you don't know."

"I need to know."

"How much do you need to know?"

"I need to know everything. I need to go very carefully these days, 'cos me and the police are not the best of friends. And that goes double if this could be dangerous. And I have a distinct feeling this whole caper could be detrimental to my health."

"I see. Well, this could take a little while."

"That's OK, 'cause I'm not phoning anyone till I'm sure I know everything I want to know."

"Now is a fine time to get tough."

"Yeah, well I've got the whisky... and I'm listening..."

Harry sat in silence until I had finished. I'll say that for him — he's a damned good listener. And when I'd finished, without speaking, he went into the kitchen and made us some tea. Still without speaking he handed me a mug and sat down.

"Where was the tea? I couldn't find any tea," I said.

He sipped quietly, ignoring me. I could tell he was thinking. Eventually he said.

"You need the magtape. You can't get any further without it. The tea was hidden in the caddie marked 'Tea', by the way."

"Well no wonder I couldn't find it. You sure? Won't the discs be enough?"

"Well who's to say the discs aren't fake, that they've not been altered? Who's to say what's on them is genuine. I mean, you found them in a wall in a house. Who put them there? Why? You can't say for sure, though you'd like to think it. No chain of evidence, as the lawyers say. In practical terms, it's gonna be bloody sight easier to read the magtape than to access these discs. Magnetic tape technology has barely changed in over thirty years."

"Which is...?"

"Very handy for us."

"Why?"

"Never mind. You need the magtape."

"I see."

"Can you get the magtape?"

"No."

"Great."

"I have a friend who can. I think."

"You think?"

"I'm fairly certain... though he might be a bit shy at first. So if I get the magtape you have a friend who can read it?"

"I think."

"You're not certain?"

"Fairly certain."

"Fairly certain he can read it?"

"No. Fairly certain they will try... if I ask."

"And once we have the magtape, what happens about the disc?"

"If you have the magtape, you don't need to worry about the disc."

"Why not?"

"Because you have the magtape."

"I see."

Reluctantly I contacted Clifford again. He was not amused and it was not a pleasant call."

"There should be a magtape copy of the disc. What I want you to do is, find the magtape."

"What the hell is magtape?"

"Something from the computer stone age, apparently. It's a magnetic tape, a copy of the material from the hard disc."

"Look I found you the log and you've located the computer disc, but I still don't know exactly what you are up to... Why are you interested in a tape?"

"Because the station log is just a log. It gives me an idea, but I need to know more. I can't get access to the discs, so..."

"So I find the tape... and then?"

"Bring it to me, of course."

"Bring? You mean you want me to nick it?"

"Borrow, Clifford. You can have it right back as soon as I'm done. Look, if I asked you to walk out of the station with the hard discs under your arm somebody would certainly notice."

"Yeah, but the amount of information on the tape, it must be...."

"Megabytes."

"Megabytes?"

"Yup."

"Meaning?"

"More information than you could shake a stick at."

"Sounds to me like you found your geek."

"Concentrate, Clifford, concentrate."

"How can you be sure no-one will notice?"

"Trust me Clifford, this stuff is garbage. They threw it to one side more than ten years ago. They probably don't even know it exists."

"I bet."

"Check it out Clifford. If you can get it, if there's no security, then you'll know I'm telling the truth."

"And if it's maximum security?"

"Just walk away."

"Well. I can do that, I reckon."

"Good man."

"OK, so tell me, then what are you looking for?"

"No idea. Just do your best. Clifford, I promise, this is the last thing I will ask, honestly."

"Well what does this magtape look like?"

"Well, it should look something like a reel of movie film, on a steel spool. It will probably be in a steel cupboard with a whole load of other magtape. It will be marked with the same file and storage code as the disc. It'll be about a foot across, maybe more, maybe less."

"You mean you don't actually know what it looks like."

"I've never seen one. They went out with the ark, practically."

"Christ. And what does it do exactly?"

"Don't ask Clifford. I can't tell you, and if I could we'd be here all night while I did. All I know is that it is very important and it should contain information crucial to this case."

"Should... probably! Could be! What kind of..."

"Clifford. Get a grip. The longer you faff about the longer you will be on the phone and the bigger the risk. Now just get on with it."

"So where am I supposed to find this magtape?"

"It'll be in the station archive. In the basement. A warm dry place, without exposure to high voltage or light."

"But this is inside a nick! The cupboard will be locked!"

"No it won't, Clifford. That's the point. I'm certain. The *discs* will be under lock and key. But nobody gives a shit about *magtape*. It's junk. They only keep it because nobody thinks to throw it away."

"You mean I can literally just walk in and pick it up?"

"Absolutely."

"And just how do you know so much about this business all of a sudden Emma?"

"I've been talking to a man who used to work there, Clifford. One of Agard's assistants."

"And how do you know the system didn't change since he was there? Just tell me. How do you know?"

"Clifford, systems don't change. Old habits don't change. I'll bet you a fiver."

Clifford, one-time Seventh Day Adventist, of good family background, cursed in a way I didn't think he knew how, and then hung up on me.

I stayed in all that night and most of the next day, sitting by the telephone. The first time it rang I nearly jumped out of my skin.

"Hello."

"This is O'Malley and O'Malley, the builders. I've had a call from your landlord. He wants me to come and look at your wall. Damp is it? Well, we need to fix a start date for the work."

"Oh, I had no idea... a start date. Right..."

"Aren't you going to ask me who's paying?"

"OK. So who's paying."

"Himself."

"The landlord?"

"Who else?" He laughed. "So you needn't worry."

I fixed a time and day with the builder, congratulating myself on having forced the landlord into doing the repairs, but my mind really was not on this triumph of diplomacy. The phone rang again. It was the vet to remind me that Beastly was overdue for his annual check up and his cat-flu shots. He should have had them weeks ago, but money had been tight. I looked at the little blighter asleep on my bed and agreed with the vet that he should have his shots as soon as possible. We pencilled in a date several weeks ahead and I hoped by that time I would be able to afford Beastly's health care. Right now I was skint as usual. Then a market research survey rang, to ask if I buy my own underwear or if my boyfriend buys it for me. I rang off before they had finished explaining. The phone rang again and I sensed it was Clifford. My hand seemed to crawl towards the phone. It was Clifford all right.

We agreed to meet at the southern cemetery gates. It looked like rain so I put on a head scarf, picked up an umbrella and folded an old plastic shopping bag into my pocket. I bought a bunch of flowers from the shop on the corner by the bus stop. Clifford was standing by his car opposite the cemetery gate. As I reached him he looked up and down the street uneasily. There was no one in sight, not even a parked car. The sky looked full of rain and a wind had sprung up. We walked quickly though the gates, past the first tall clump of bushes, in among the crooked gravestones, and took up a position under a cypress tree. We stood looking at the grave of someone called Bertha Mullendorf. The stone read:

Grandmother of dear memory,
born 1801, died 1898.
Gone to be a Sunbeam.

"Sunbeam," I said. "At her age? You got it?"

"I got it."

"And?"

"No problem."

"Just like I said?"

"Just like you said."

"Tell me."

"It's a spool of film in a tin can. All neatly labelled, with a date and everything. The same file code as the discs. It was sat in an unlocked steel cupboard, in the corridor outside the station archive. Not even inside, for God's sake. I can't believe it."

"Anybody see you?"

"One of the archivists."

"Male or female, Clifford."

"What's it matter?"

"Male or female?"

"Female."

"Did she ask what you were doing?"

"Not exactly. I just said I was looking for space to store some stuff."

"Nice and vague."

"She didn't bat an eyelid. What kind of security is this?"

"Well done Clifford. So my source was sound. Maybe next time you'll take my word."

"There ain't gonna be no next time."

"Cliffie... and just when you were doing so well."

"Don't make a joke out of it. I reckon they're on to me. My phone sounds funny. There's a car parked at the end of my street."

"But you got away with the tape... speaking of which..."

With a quick glance around, Clifford slipped the can of tape from inside his coat into my carrier bag. He frowned.

"Did it never occur to you, they wanted me to get away with the tape? Did it never occur to you, they want to know what we want to know?"

"What?"

"They could have led us on."

"They, Clifford?"

"Christ!"

"Clifford, are you telling me we've been set up for something? For what? What good would we be? We don't even know what we're looking for yet."

"True. But then, you knew you wanted to get the tape, which was probably more than they knew. We might not recognise the evidence when we find it. But they will. I'm not certain how they'd know, but... Look... I feel I've got eyes all over me. My skin is crawling, like I'm itching. I got a rash, a nervous rash. Somebody is watching me. Maybe not all the time, but somebody has their eye on me. I can feel it."

"Clifford, we're on to something... something...."

"Something…. something that could get us killed. I got a wife…"

"And a kid on the way. I've heard the record. I won't ask you for anything else Clifford, honest."

"And we shouldn't meet anymore either."

"Right. So I suppose a lift back to Withington is out of the question."

Clifford ran from the cemetery. I placed my flowers across Bertha Mullendorf's grave and turned to follow. Clifford got into his car and drove off. As he did a heavy rain began, gusting down from the north towards the motorway, bayonets dancing on the street. Almost immediately the gutters were full to overflowing. As Clifford's car turned the corner a large family saloon, which must have parked down the street while we were under the cypress tree, started up. I noticed its lights come on. It pulled out into the road. I ducked back behind the stone pillar of the cemetery gates. The car drove slowly past me, I glimpsed a young man at the wheel, an old man clutching flowers sat in the passenger seat, both were staring forwards into the rain. They drove round the corner, the same way Clifford had gone. I thought if they bought flowers to put on a grave, why are they driving away with them?

I had to wait for ages for the bus. All the glass in the bus shelter had been smashed, so the wind whistled through it, carrying a fine spray of rain. I was drenched. I wanted to get out of my wet shoes as quickly as possible, but I decided to ring Harry from the call box on the corner before I went home.

"Hi," he said. "Got anything for me yet?"

"Well, I've been shopping and I just got hold of a really interesting tape."

"Would I like it?"

"Oh I think it's exactly your kind of thing."

"So let's meet and listen to it together. Say, about fifteen minutes?"

I just had time to change my shoes. The rain eased off. I waited outside clutching the carrier bag. Lace curtains on the ground floor flat twitched. Harry raced up well inside fifteen minutes and came to a halt with a squeal of brakes. I should have known. Harry was driving a bright pink Triumph sports model with a soft top. The soft top had been sliced open. The seats were soaking wet. Harry gallantly spread a black plastic bin liner over the seat for me.

"Some charming bleeder did this last night."

"Vandals?"

"I doubt it. And so do you. Look, it's all nice and neat. This was a professional villain with a very sharp chiv, not some punk with a pen knife."

"Clifford thinks he's being watched."

"I see."

"And I think he's being followed."

"Then he probably is."

"They were after whatever we've got, I reckon."

"Did they get anything from the car? Where were the discs?"

"They didn't take anything."

"Nothing?"

"No, not a thing. But, what's peculiar is, the discs were sat on the back seat."

"Eh?"

"I don't think they knew what they were looking for."

"Let's hope it stays that way. Where are we going?"

"An old friend from my university days."

"You went to university?"

"Yup."

"And you've got a friend."

"Ain't life strange?"

"And this friend agreed to help?"

"Absolutely."

"So you didn't tell him everything?"

"Not everything."

"So what did you say?"

"No more than I had to. I said it's a bit hush-hush. I said, I'm definitely on the right side of the law, this time, but it's still a bit... delicate."

"You have such a way with words Harry."

We drove on in silence. I got the distinct impression Harry had done this kind of thing before.

Chronology: 5 October 1988

Pinochet brought in his own economists — Chilean mone-tarists who had trained at the University of Chicago. They promptly dismantled all the social programmes set up by Allende and assisted in the destruction of the Chilean Trade Unions. Between 1972 and 1982 GNP per capita fell by 6.4% and as the economy plunged into general poverty, the giant US corporations in Chile repeatedly lowered wages.

General Pinochet, defeated in the national plebiscite of 1988, finally agreed to resign from the Presidency, but only on condition that he was allowed to reserve for himself the post of Head of the Chilean Armed Forces. Before leaving office he granted himself perpetual immunity from all prosecution. However, on 8 December 1988 UN Convention against Torture came into effect.

Jaime Perez-Cervera & Maria-Dolores Jamon
Augusto: The Little Book of the General

We started the drive into central Manchester on the end of the rush hour traffic. It was already dark and the last of the sunset clouds formed a brilliant orange and purple map across the sky. We drove on in silence, past Platt Fields, the curry strip of Rusholme, where the aroma of spices formed a different kind of cloud, then on past closed down cloth shops and warehouses, past a car showroom and Victoria Park, then the Manchester Royal Infirmary. Ahead of us red rear lights made a ruby dragon's tail into the city.

I suddenly realised I was very, very tired. I was also cold and damp.

We stopped at the traffic lights opposite Contact Theatre. Harry looked at the theatre and shook his head.

"I got nothing against blind people, but they didn't oughter design buildings."

"Where exactly are you taking me Harry?"

"Told you. To see an old friend."

We turned into a side road and parked at the back of the University.

"University?"

"And why not? They have computers too, you know. You got the magtape?"

We threaded our way through a maze of buildings until we reached a long, low, crumbling Nissen hut set in what looked like a waste land of wild fruit bushes and lumpy grass. The hut was dwarfed by tall modern buildings on every side. I noticed there were heavy bars and shutters on the windows, and CCTV cameras trained along the frontage. Harry led the way inside. The light was bright in the corridor. Harry knocked on a door and a voice inside answered.

"Hang on here a moment," said Harry and disappeared into the office. I noticed the name of a Professor Zajac on the door. I could hear voices inside. Sounded like Harry was having to explain himself. It was warm in the corridor. I began to steam. After about fifteen minutes the door opened and Harry beckoned me into the office.

"I'd like to introduce you to Professor Zajac."

Harry stepped back to reveal a desk covered with papers, and behind the desk was a tall shapely blonde woman. We shook hands.

"I don't know why, but I was expecting a man."

"Don't worry. I earned my post the hard way."

"The Professor was my teacher... once," said Harry.

"Harry was just about my best ever student. He could have got a university post easily, but..."

"Not for me, really."

"No, not for Harry. He preferred something a little more exciting... the possibility of big bucks."

"Which could explain why he's permanently broke," I said.

"Don't let that little council house with the peeling woodwork fool you. Harry is the best in the business.

Everybody knows that. Even my best graduate students contact Harry. I reckon he's probably got millions stashed away in some Swiss bank account."

"I wish," laughed Harry, not in the least bit convincing.

"All done electronically, of course. The only problem is that he does keep straying onto the wrong side of the law... don't you Harry?"

"Come on you two. No ganging up. Is it my fault? I ask you, is it my fault if the law cannot keep up with technology?"

"Hacking into the BUPA computer to get Mrs Thatcher's medical record is not a slight lag in technology law."

"It was a grey area."

"No. It was an out-and-out invasion of privacy."

"OK, all right. I'll give you that one. But it was in a good cause."

"Agreed. And the papers paid you a small fortune."

"So I got caught. So I did a little time. It was worth it just for the look on her face when the news broke."

"And it didn't do your bank balance any harm either. Did they track the money down?"

"Nope."

"So that explains the 'poor act'. Very smart Harry. Very smart."

"It's not an act. They confiscated everything they could find."

"What I really want to know is, Harry, what have you got for me this time?"

"It's a beauty," said Harry and nodded to me.

I hauled the reel of magtape out of the plastic carrier bag and laid it on the desk.

"Where did you get *that?*" said Zajac.

"I'd prefer not to say at this stage... but it's nothing to do with BUPA I swear."

"And what do you want me to do with it?"

"Well, I'd like you to transfer everything on the tape onto floppy disc."

"Not one disc. More like twenty, maybe thirty, I'd say."

"That's OK. I brought a box of twenty-four with me. Should be enough, eh?"

"Twenty-four? Sounds like quite a night. And why have you brought this to me?"

"It's your mainframe," said Harry.

"My mainframe?"

"Size."

"Well, it is important." The Professor and I exchanged glances.

"So I've heard. Anyway, since the police confiscated my stuff after the BUPA do, I haven't been able to replace it. I mean I have to take my time or they'll get suspicious, you know. What I've got at the moment just isn't big enough. Also, to be honest, I need something, well, a little... older... than my current set up."

"You mean you can't read it, if I put it straight onto floppy disc. You also want this translated into a more accessible language? Harry, this is gonna cost you. Big time."

"Absolutely."

"I mean, at least a film, dinner, champagne, flowers, chocolates, breakfast in bed — oysters and more champagne..."

"Anything."

"In Paris. Hmm. You agree? So, it's that big?" said the Professor.

"That big."

"I see."

"So say it."

"The works."

"I promise."

"I promise the works, but afterwards."

"OK. And I've got a witness, right?" She nodded at me, smiling.

Professor Zajac led the way out of the office and down the corridor. She unlocked a room and ushered us inside. The room was packed with huge machines almost as high

97

as the ceiling. Tubes and valves glowed in the dark. There was a smell of ozone.

"You are in the presence of history. These are some of the oldest surviving bits of Alan Turing's original set up. Turing? Don't suppose the name rings any bells for you…"

"Alan Turing," I said, dredging my memory. "Mathematician. One of the founders of modern computing. Best remembered for his work on breaking the German Enigma codes at Bletchley Park during World War Two… used to live not far from me, on Palatine Road. His private life was a bit of a mess. Unhappy man. Nowadays he would probably fit right in."

"I'm impressed."

"I'm a fund of useless information. Hazard of the profession."

"Which is?"

"Journalism."

"How long will this take?" said Harry. I think he was irritated that I was chatting with the Professor.

"Copying the tape onto our hard disc is slow going. It will take about two hours, at least."

The Professor turned towards me.

"Your clothes are steaming and that's bad for the machinery. Very sensitive to humidity. Why don't you two go and get a cup of coffee while I set this up. Have you eaten? Better get something. After that, Harry, I'm afraid you will have to lend a hand."

"Yeah. What d'you want me to do?"

"Well, the stuff on the tape can be transferred onto disc, no problem, but we will have to find a language that's compatible with yours, which means I might have to translate everything into one or two intervening languages before I get one that your machine can access. Then you will need to copy your final version onto floppy discs so that you can take it away with you."

"And that is my task?"

"Right. Me and my mainframe get all the neat stuff, and you get all the drudgery. There's a good vegetarian place

98

just down the road, called The Eighth Day. This could be a long night. Come back at about nine o' clock."

We found The Eighth Day Cafe without any difficulty.

"Harry," I said. "tell me about this breakfast in bed thing."

"Er, well, me and the Professor are…"

"An item?"

"Old friends."

"She's a beauty Harry."

"I know. And smart as a whip."

"Are you sure?"

"How d'you mean?"

"Well she likes you Harry. How smart is that?"

"Some women are funny feeders."

"You said it."

"She likes me for my mind."

"I bet she does."

"No, honest."

"I believe you, Harry. Nevertheless, you are a dark horse. I have to regard you in an entirely different light."

"And… and is that good or… bad?"

"Well, I'll have to remove you from my possibles list. And now you're definitely off my probables list."

"So where will you put me?"

"Oh, one of my other lists."

"How many lists have you got?"

"That, Harry, would be telling. Now, how d'you fancy a sesame tofu burger?"

"Nah, I fancy a nice cup of tea and sausage roll."

"Harry, this is a vegetarian cafe."

Chronology: April 1990-March 1991

The Rettig Commission for Truth and Reconciliation was set up by order of new Chilean President, Patricio Aylwin. This Commission was ordered to report on human rights abuses resulting in death under General Pinochet's regime. The Retting Commission reported in March 1991 and its findings shocked Chilean polite society with a powerful collection of research and personal testimony. The report outlined 2,279 deaths which were the responsibility of the state security services — police, armed forces, intelligence services and DINA [secret police]. The commission mentioned a further 508 cases which it knew about but had not been able to investigate, mentioned 449 names of individuals about whom it had been unable to uncover any information and listed 957 victims who had disappeared without trace. But this was only a preliminary survey.

Jaime Perez-Cervera & Maria-Dolores Jamon
Augusto: The Little Book of the General

Harry rang my door bell at about seven in the morning. I let him in.

"I've got the discs."

"How many?"

"In all, twenty-four. But apart from that I was thinking about Miller. Just a chance, you know, but I thought I'd see if I could access the staff list at the Non-Ferrous Metals Information Service, where Miller worked, see if I could find a few names, you know."

"How would you do that, Harry?"

"A technical matter really."

"Is it legal?"

"Yeah... well, all right. Technical and legal."

"Answer the question Harry. Is it legal?"

"Well, yes, it's relatively legal."

"How relative is relative?"

"Well, it's more legal than, say, assassinating the US president. You gotta have perspective on these things. It ain't like its genocide or incest or robbing the blind is it?"

"All right Harry, I think I can fill in the rest of the argument for myself. Fine. Just let me know when you get something, will you?"

"That's what I'm doing. I already done the deed."

"Bloody hell, Harry. You don't hang about do you?"

"No, well copying those bloody discs backwards and

100

forwards is real boring, so while I was waiting I used the facilities."

"So, what did you get?"

"I got two names. A chap called Guido Cyprianou, deputy director of the Non-Ferrous Metals Information Service, and a chap by the name of Solomon Da Silva. And what do you know? Da Silva was Miller's old boss, and he only pops up in the papers this morning, doesn't he? Look."

Harry spread a newspaper out on the breakfast table, tapping at a photograph."

"Da Silva."

"And he is?"

"Only the bloody President of the Non-Ferrous Metals Information Service. MBE and all."

"And what's he in the papers for?"

"Supposed to go to Buck House this morning to pick up his K."

"His what?"

"His K. A knighthood. Services to Industry and all that."

"And?"

"Only went and had a heart attack last night, didn't he?"

"Dead?"

"Not quite dead enough to be really dead. More sort of lingering."

"So where is he now?"

"In the King David Hospital — private job. Jewish."

"I'll get down there. You never know, maybe I can wangle a chat."

"A chat? About what?"

"Maybe he can tell me something about Miller."

"In hospital?"

"Where else am I going to get anywhere near him?"

"Better hurry, then. Says here it was his third major heart attack and his wife says: 'surgery after his last illness was not as successful as we had hoped'. Sounds like he's about to pop his clogs. Could be a death bed confession."

"Well done, Harry. Nice one. Not just a hacker are you?"

"You ain't seen nothing yet, doll."

"I know, and I'm not sure I want to."

I had expected tighter security. I told them I was a journalist, flashed them my union card, said I was meeting Da Silva's family for an extended interview, that they were preparing for the worst and wanted good coverage with the obituary. They all seemed happy with that. The Ward Sister said the family would be arriving shortly and that I should wait in the anteroom. I pulled out a magazine and pretended to read. As soon as the Staff Nurse went around the corner I put the magazine on the seat as if I had just gone to the bathroom and would be back in a moment, and then shot into the private room beyond.

The blinds were drawn. Solomon Da Silva MBE lay on his bed surrounded by drip stands, monitors, flashing lights, trailing wires. He was old: very, very old. There was a smell. He smelled like he was dying. I just hoped he still had all his marbles and that he could still talk. Softly I called out his name: "Solomon... Solomon Da Silva."

He opened his eyes.

"Mr Da Silva... Solomon... Don't be alarmed. I'm a journalist. I'm writing a piece about you for the papers. I want to ask a few questions."

"What? About what? My obituary? Ask my wife." His breath hissed.

"Yes. OK. I'll do that. But I also wanted to ask you about a man called Miller. Remember Miller? He used to work for you. At the Non-Ferrous Metals Information Service."

"Miller."

"The one that died. In the shooting."

"You're not writing my obituary."

"Yes, I am. I want to. But after this, OK? Just answer the questions, Mr Da Silva. If you feel poorly I will leave immediately."

102

"Sweetheart. I'm dying. I'm not likely to feel better than this for some... considerable time."

"I'm very sorry to hear that."

"I'm not. But you managed to get in here... you got past them... you have questions... and I'm in the mood. And none of it matters to me any more. Ask your questions, pretty lady. Ask."

"Well. OK. so what happened to Miller?"

"Miller? I fired him."

"Why? What for?"

"He stole."

"Money?"

"Information."

"About what?"

"He should never have seen the stuff. He wasn't cleared."

"What do you mean? Explain, please Solomon. Please explain."

"It's all on record."

"I have no access to the records. If you don't tell me no-one will ever know. Tell me please, Solomon."

"The CIA. Their fault. It was a mistake. Because Miller was working on copper... the idiots put him on a circulation list. Documents relating to Chile, Allende, CIA plans for Chile. He saw them all. If I had realised..."

"And what was in the documents?"

"Plans. Press releases. Announcements. Draft texts... for public... release."

"So?"

"Don't you see?"

"No. No I don't."

"Everything... everything was prepared... more than two years before... the coup... before Allende died. The announcement... of Allende's death... everything. It was... all prepared... in advance... Do you see now? I mean Allende had to die."

"So Miller saw CIA documents? At the Information Service? Is that it? Is that a yes, Soloman? Did Miller see secret CIA documents?"

"Yes."

"And when you reported it."

"When I reported it... Miller..."

"Miller was killed."

"I never meant for him to die. The Chilean secret service... crude, brutal, bastards."

"And the CIA covered it up by making sure the police investigation into Miller's death failed."

"Yes."

"What about Agard? Where does he fit into all this?"

"Never heard of him."

"Why didn't you tell anyone about what happened to Miller?"

"Why?"

"Doesn't right and wrong interest you?"

"You are not my rabbi."

"Right."

"I have a wife... children... Who could I tell?"

"What about the police?"

"You... joke... no?"

"The newspapers, TV, your MP."

"So who will you tell?"

"Someone. Anyone... But not your rabbi, if that's what worries you."

"Promise."

"I promise not to tell your rabbi."

"No. Promise to... tell them... everyone..."

"What, even the rabbi?"

"All."

"OK, but you can kiss your knighthood goodbye."

His breath was suddenly laboured, his face puffy, his eyes were yellow and bloodshot. He hissed.

"I am... ashamed... I liked Miller. I liked him. Tell everyone. But... Take care... Chile... You."

His last word was a long drawn out sigh. His eyelids flickered and then his eyeballs rolled up to show the yellowed whites. The monitor beside the bed ceased beeping and began to emit a single tone. I backed away from the

104

bed and quickly ducked back into the anteroom as if I had never bothered the man, as if nothing at all had happened.

When the hospital emergency team rushed in with their trolley full of equipment and tanks of oxygen I folded away my magazine, did my best to look surprised and alarmed. The nurse moved into my path, as if to bar the door to the inner room.

"I am sorry," she said firmly. "but I think you had better come back another time."

"I quite understand. Is it very bad?"

"I can't say. It's not good. Come back later, eh?"

Next morning the builders turned up on my doorstep at eight o'clock in the morning. Luckily I was up and dressed.

"I thought we agreed next week?"

"No. This week. Look I have it written down... well somewhere..." He rummaged in his pockets bringing out crumpled pieces of paper in his enormous hands. "Anyway your landlord is paying, so I'd take it while you can. We're here now, so let's make a start."

They poked the walls with little pointy gadgets, and took readings from meters, all the while looking serious and tutt-tutting. Then they started to bring in bags of tools, and one of them went off to crawl about in the roof space. Eventually they conferred and Mr O'Malley came so speak with me.

"We'll only be in your kitchen and your loo. After that you can leave us get on with it. We have a front door key from your landlord, so if you give us a key to the flat access won't be a problem. Now you've got several problems here: a broken pipe, rising damp, descending damp, dry rot, dead squirrels, blocked gutters. Oh, and missing tiles. You're landlord should have taken action years ago, but now the damage means we're going to take down most of that wall and rebuild it, and we're going to have to do something about your rafters too. It's only pigeon shit holding the place together, if you'll pardon the expression."

He reached up and pushed his hand into the plaster of the kitchen wall. It crumbled under his fingers, and as he pushed I could see the brickwork moving.

"This is far worse than I had thought."

"One bad storm and you'd have woken up in the street."

We agreed that I would move my kitchen stuff into the bedroom. I locked Beastly in the bedroom and put Maggie and Adolf in the bathroom. Then I tacked up a couple of dust sheets over the doors, and laid newspapers on the floor in the hall to try and minimise the mess. By lunch time the builders had erected a scaffold along the side of the house, had begun to put up Acro-props from floor to ceiling in the kitchen and I had made several pots of very strong tea.

I went to the phone box on the corner and rang Clough. I said there had been a couple of developments and asked if he wanted to see what we had so far. He said he had some material of his own to show us. But his car was in the garage for its MOT, he explained, so he would come over tomorrow on the train.

Next day I got to Harry's place about 10.30am. I crumpled onto the sofa, propping my red and bleary eyes wide open with my fingertips.

"Tea?"

"It'll take more than tea, Harry."

"Breakfast?"

"No ta. I want my home back. I want a bath. I want bed. But my place is a tip. Dirt and dust everywhere."

"You really have to tidy up more often Emma."

"Yeah, right. It's conference time. Let's pool our information and see what we've got. I've got a friend meeting us here, Harry."

"I thought I was your friend."

"My other friend."

"You got two friends. You bloody show off you."

"And in the meantime, there's just one thing."

Harry sighed. "Yeah and I know just what it isn't."

"Now then Harry, let's not make the Professor jealous."

"I knew you'd hold her against me."

"You wish. Look, I want you to make copies of the discs."

"What? All of 'em?"

"Insurance. If anything happens, I want copies out there, in the world. I want the story known."

"The story?"

"Well, as much of it as we can piece together, anyway."

Harry sighed, reached under his table and brought out a large box of blank computer discs. "Right. So how many copies d'you want? Three? And who's paying for the discs?"

Clough was one of those people who prided himself on being punctual. The train must have been on time — with Clough on board it probably didn't dare run late. Warily Harry shook hands with Clough, eyeing his green silk wind-cheater and orange baseball cap. Harry decided he needed a lie-down. Well why not? Harry had done a load of brain work on the computer, setting everything up for me to read. So maybe he'd earned a little nap.

He stretched out on the sofa and went right off to sleep. I explained to Clough what I had found at the house and told him about the meeting in London with the civilian computer expert from Agard's old station team. Then I explained about the magtape and the professor. Harry was snoring gently in the background. Clough listened carefully, smiling. Then he took off his jacket and draped it over the back of a chair.

"So do you have a print out, or do we have to scroll through everything on-screen."

"As yet, it's all on screen, I'm afraid. Harry has set it up for us."

"Comfy chair too, I hope." We set to work. It took more than three hours to read all the relevant case files from the disc. By the time we had finished Harry was awake again. Clough asked Harry some technical questions, ending with: "So let me get this straight. This material is from the magtape copy of the police disc that Agard changed, before the disc he put in was itself replaced, possibly by this Yank military type?"

"Right."

"And you have the original disc."

"We do, but for technical reasons we can't get into it. We could solve that in time."

"But going for the magtape was the next best option because no one thought to lock it up, and if no-one thought to lock it up then they probably didn't think to tamper with it either."

"Right, but the magtape is actually better than any disc, for our purposes, anyway."

"Why's that?"

"Because unlike a disc, you can't overwrite magtape. Precisely because it's a tape it can't be tampered with."

Clough smiled, rubbed his eyes and said he needed to go for a run to clear his head. He took his bag into the bathroom and changed into a snazzy light grey and silver track suit. Then, humming quietly he launched himself out of the front door at a speed nothing short of remarkable for man of his years. Harry was impressed.

"Keeps himself very trim and fit, does your Chief Inspector Clough."

"I think he calls himself Mr Clough these days."

"Maybe, but it's definitely a healthy mind in a healthy body, as the old Romans used to say. Nice bloke, but he is a bit."

"A bit what?"

"Well, stylistically challenged."

"Harry, I want you to do something for me."

"Yeah? What?"

"I want you to stand in front of your wardrobe for five minutes... with the doors open. You do have a wardrobe... Harry... Harry?"

When Clough got back from his run he took a shower. I went out and bought us all a nice Chinese take away. And rather than waste time trying to chip the dirt off Harry's crockery I invested in chop sticks, paper plates and plastic cups from the corner shop.

Harry and Clough seemed to be getting on OK. But I could sense that Harry was uneasy around the ex-policeman. I put that down to natural caution and plain old guilt. I also felt that he was curious about my relationship with Clough. Clough came down from the bathroom with his hair still dripping, dressed again in his emerald green silk wind-cheater and orange baseball cap.

"That's better. Nearly human again."

I doled out rice and noodles. Harry opened up the other containers.

"I think I should start by telling you what Da Silva told me."

"That's a good place to start. Go right ahead."

They listened in silence while I went through my notes of the conversation. Finally Clough, waved a chop stick in the air.

"The way I see it, is this. Without a doubt, Agard bricked up the discs for safe keeping. It was probably for the discs that Agard and Miller were killed."

"And the paper boy," said Harry.

"And the paper boy, of course," agreed Clough.

"So," said Harry. "It would seem that the Yank, who was probably CIA rather than military, doctored the disc without realising that Agard had just changed it and that Agard had kept both the original disc and the magtape copy."

"OK. Agreed," I said. "But why would they need to doctor the disc?"

"Aha, I thought about that," said Harry, tapping the screen with his chop stick. "I think the answer is in these case files here. And in the SATLog file."

Clough leaned forward and wiped soy sauce from the screen with his paper napkin.

Clough looked at Harry. A moment of tension. It was Harry's computer. He could splash it with soy sauce if he wanted to. He could smear it with peanut butter for all I cared.

"What's a SATLog?" I said.

"Station Automatic Telephone Log," said Clough. "It lists all phone calls in and out of the nick. If you look…"

Clough tapped keys and the screen changed.

"If you look here you'll see we have a complete list of phone numbers and locations, all identified and authenticated with a special Home Office code. And the log shows that on the night Agard upgraded the disc, our Chief Inspector received a phone call from the Chief Constable, followed by a phone call from the Home Office, followed by a phone call from Downing Street."

"But why?"

Clough studied the screen a moment. "I'm guessing, but I'd say they were leaning on the Chief Constable to find a way of dropping the case. Warning him they were sending someone to look at the computer files. I'd say they gave him no choice, probably called it a matter of national importance. Look there's even a call here from the Ministry of Defence."

Harry leaned in closer to the screen to get a better look and then said quietly: "But this call. It's from…"

"Quite right. A personal call from the very highest in the land — next to the Queen Mum of course."

"Harry, how do you know that? It's just a number."

Harry shrugged.

"I just know. I recognise several of these numbers. They sometimes come up."

"In the normal course of your work?"

"You could say that."

"Well, this is clearly something big," I said. "But what?"

"Yeah," said Harry, looking at Clough. "You were in charge. So come on, you tell us what it means."

"I wish I knew," said Clough. "These calls were not to me, remember. I knew nothing about them until just now. All I know is that the day after these calls came in there was an American in the computer room putting right a problem none of our technicians knew about. The same day I was retired. And shortly after that Agard

110

disappeared. And then the case was quietly dropped."

"OK. So is there anything else here?"

"There is." Clough tapped the keys again. "It was important to doctor the case files and the phone log. We can assume that was what the Yank was doing. We can also assume he deleted or changed evidence files from the case too. Look. This file is one we opened regarding possible motives for the torture and murder of Miller. We have all the normal lists of possibilities — sexual jealousy, revenge, ex-wife, girl friend, rival, drugs, criminal connections, inheritance problems, possible homosexual connections... But the one that has come to interest me since then was thought a bit of a red herring at the time. Possible political connections: membership of political parties, student activities, social connections, and so on. Now this file was due for review at a Case Conference the day after they forced me out, so I never actually got to see the information in the full file. But here, and I'm seeing this file for the first time remember, we can see Miller worked as a statistician for the Non-Ferrous Metals Information Service."

"But you knew this before, surely, it was no secret that he worked for a living."

"True."

"So? Is there a political connection there? How?"

"Yes, we knew where he worked. And we knew he was a statistician, and that he specialised in copper. But that was all. You see, the whole function of files like this is to order the information you have and to show it in another light. We were just about to consider whether his work could have provided a motive for his death."

"So what do you think the connection might have been?"

"I've often wondered. When I was retired I had lots of time on my hands — I hadn't expected to go for quite a while. I'd made no preparations, no hobbies, you know. But then I'd got a bit of money in the bank, and suddenly a police pension. So I decided to travel a bit. I went on a

111

group tour of South America — I'd always wanted to go there. I could have gone to South Africa or Canada, Australia, but I wanted something else... can't say what exactly. Anyway I had a great time. I went to all those ancient Aztec and Inca sights, pyramids and buried cities in the jungle and up into the mountains to see Matchu Pitchu, the city in the clouds. Incredible places. Wonderful. Got mugged. Got diarrhoea so bad... Montezuma's revenge they call it. And everybody there is so small, I felt like a giant, you know? I really fell in love with the place. I could show you pictures."

I think he saw the look on our faces.

"Well... maybe another time, eh? And when I got back I started to read up on things. I even took an Open University course. And while I was reading about South America, quite by accident, I stumbled onto a possible connection. Part of Miller's job at the Non-Ferrous Metals Information Service had been to comb the trade and business journals, financial papers, published company reports and so on, to compile a dossier of information and statistics on mined, smelted and refined copper production world-wide. Ostensibly he was to do this for the metals industry as a whole. The copper industry was badly hit in the late 1960s, with the introduction of plastic tubing and piping, and they were keen to smooth things out in future, as far as they could. So they wanted to be able to predict production and prices. They wanted near perfect knowledge: supplies, amounts of copper, availability, the likely price."

"But? There is a 'but'?"

"A very big but."

"The Non-Ferrous Metals Information Service was funded by the British metals industry and..."

"And, let me guess... the CIA?"

"Got it. The CIA. This little gem emerged recently, courtesy of the US Freedom of Information Act."

"But why would they be interested in copper?"

"They weren't interested in copper as such. Information

112

that affects the world economy was — is — very useful to the CIA. It points out likely trouble spots, and helps stabilise US industry."

"Is US interest in copper big?" I asked.

"Absolutely enormous," said Harry. "And the US has always been very touchy about South America, you know about allowing communism to get a toehold so close to home. They regard it as their personal backyard. President Nixon was obsessed with the idea that the communists were going to invade through Mexico. President Jimmy Carter tried to clean things up, you know, improve the Human Rights angle. But when Reagan was elected President in 1981 the first thing he did was order a 'Security Policy Review' in South America. And all Carter's Human Rights stuff just went out the window. It was back to business as usual."

"I'm beginning to see a picture emerge here."

"Good," said Clough. "So back in the early 1970s there was a crisis. The newly elected Chilean President Allende was a socialist. As soon as he got into power he started to nationalise the Chilean copper industry, mines, smelters and refineries, mostly owned by US companies."

"When you say US interest in the copper industry was absolutely enormous... how absolutely enormous is that absolutely enormous?"

"I mean absolutely enormously enormous. The world's largest underground copper mine and the world's largest open cast copper mines are both in Chile. If you look at the US-owned open cast mine at Chuquicamata, the pit is about as wide across as the city of Coventry. It is so deep there are sections at the bottom of the pit in almost permanent shadow, except for a few minutes at midday. You could stand the Empire State building in the crater and it would not reach near the top; astronauts can see it from space. They say it is just a huge black hole."

"I can see why the CIA would be interested."

"There is more. President Allende not only nationalised the mines, he presented the Yanks with a huge bill, saying

113

that as the profit made from the mines had been taken out of the country and had never been spent or invested in Chile, the Americans had damaged the health and wealth not only of the copper workers, but just about everyone in the country. Of course Allende was absolutely right, but all this was happening just as the US companies in Chile were poised to bring on-line huge expansions in ore production. These expansions would have made Chile the biggest copper source in the world. The beauty of this expansion, from a US point of view, was that the copper ore and the profits went directly to the US. The ore would be smelted and refined in the US and the money would be spent in the US. Apart from wages, there was very little leakage of finance or profit into the Chilean economy. The CIA could not afford to lose control of Chilean copper production, let alone get stuck with a bill for damages going back nearly a hundred years."

"But hang on," I said. "None of this is secret, is it? I mean it was in the newspapers, it was available to the public. I mean, if you could read, you could know all about this."

"Sure, you could. But I don't think Miller and the kid were killed for that information. This is the context of the crime. They were killed for something else, something connected to this information."

"Like what?"

"Well, I don't know for sure, but I have an idea."

"Spit it out."

Harry groaned loudly. "A bottle of scotch is not going to be enough."

"What?"

"If I had known it was going to be this big, I would have demanded a crate of Scotch."

"Speaking of which, Harry, how about a drink?"

"What, you want to drink my profits now?"

I got out the plastic cups. Harry brought ice in a breakfast bowl from the fridge and then grudgingly poured us a very slim finger of whisky each.

114

"So come on," I said spooning more ice into my cup. "What kind of thing is this? I mean it's already a bit thick for a provincial hack."

"And for a provincial hacker," said Harry, stirring the whisky with his finger.

"No less so for a broken old hack like me," said Clough, sipping and savouring the whisky. He thought a moment and then resumed.

"Think about what eventually happened. General Pinochet, the Army Chief of Staff, led a military coup. The Presidential Palace was bombed. Allende was killed. Pinochet stopped the nationalisation of the mines, restored US influence, passed all opposition off as communist, killed and tortured thousands. And he did this with the support of the CIA."

"So the CIA helped stage the coup?"

"They deny it of course. They say it was all Pinochet's handiwork, they only offered him their support after the coup was successful. But the evidence is overwhelming. And they justified their support of Pinochet by saying Allende had been elected on a minority vote, that he had no popular mandate."

"Hang on," said Harry. "That's normal. I mean even with the first past the post system it's absolutely normal for a government to be larger than its nearest rival, but smaller than the total of the opposition parties. Statistically that's spot on for almost any modern democracy."

"That's right. Mrs Thatcher has about the same percentage vote as Allende, even at her most successful."

"Funny, I didn't notice the CIA riding in to rescue us," I said

"Very selective, the CIA."

"Bump off your enemies, sir. It'll be a pleasure," said Harry.

"Listen. Agard's reappearance might have triggered something, but I think the real answer to this puzzle is going to be with Miller."

"Yes, we have a lot of stuff that indicates a connection to him," said Harry.

"I think he's some kind of catalyst. But, what we don't have is something that directly connects Miller and Agard."

"And Chile," I said.

"And Chile," Harry echoed.

"Maybe we just have to be patient and keep on plugging."

"Yeah we got this far... something will turn up."

"I don't mind something turning up. I just hope it's not the CIA."

"I have a few ideas. I'm going over to Liverpool tomorrow, so with a bit of luck I'll see you in a couple of days," said Clough.

"Can I ask you a question?"

"Of course. Ask any question you like, Emma. You might not like the answer, but you can ask. What is it?"

"Well, you could just sit back and let me do the necessary at this stage. I mean, you could feed me stuff, ideas, contacts, where to look next, that kind of thing. Let me do the legwork. I mean that must have been what you did on the force, a lot of the time. But you're not going to, are you? Why? What's in it for you?"

"You think it's gone, it's in the past, that I should let it go?" Clough replied.

"Maybe... you're retired."

"And at my age, what? It's foolish for me to try to sort this out?"

"Maybe."

"Maybe, maybe."

"All I'm saying is that neither of you need be involved any further. If you want to back out now, that would be OK with me, really," I said.

"Why are you saying that Emma?"

"Because if what we have just put together is right, then we are messing with some very nasty people."

***

I went home for a bath feeling vaguely guilty that I could not remember when I had last fed Beastly. The mess in the kitchen did not bear looking at. So I didn't. I could hear the plastic sheeting covering the side of the house flapping gently in the breeze. The flat was cold and there was a fine film of grit everywhere. Well, at least Beastly was still there. He hissed a welcome at me before settling in to scoff a tin of cat food, growling and muttering to himself and eyeing me as if I were about to snatch it away from him. Maggie and Adolf didn't complain or hiss, so I gave them a double helping of ant eggs and headed for bed.

Chronology: 1992-1996

In 1992 US President George Bush pardoned ex-President Ronald Reagan, ex-Secretary of Defence Caspar Weinberger and five other senior members of the Reagan administration. The crimes they were pardoned for were never specified. George Bush had been Vice President throughout Ronald Reagan's term in office and had been charged with special responsibility for overseeing CIA activities. He had been party to all Reagan's decisions on Chile. Neither Reagan nor Bush has ever been brought to trial for the destruction of Chilean democracy, an operation which had no mandate from the US electorate, which subverted US tax dollars and which broke international law. What was the difference between this and General Pinochet offering himself immunity from prosecution?

On the recommendation of the Rettig Commission, the Chilean Reparation and Reconciliation Commission was set up. The mandate of this new commission was extended several times over the next four years. In January 1996 the Reparation and Conciliation Commission reported that it had investigated 641 cases which the Rettig Commission had been unable to resolve, 123 disappearances that came to light after the Rettig Commission ceased to operate and a further 776 extrajudicial executions and killings by torture — all committed by the military. At this point the number of cases against the Pinochet regime were thought to be 2,095 known killings and a further 1,102 'disappearances'. While these figures fell well below some of estimates of 'massacre', it was later raised to 3,100 known deaths.

Next morning the builders got me out of bed at 7.30am.

"It's still dark," I protested. They smiled, switched on the kitchen lights and set to work. I went back to bed, but they had a radio playing pop tunes at full blast. After about half an hour one of them came knocking on my bedroom door.

"You want a cup of tea, luv?"

"Sure. Why not?"

I decided it was a risk, but I needed to contact Clifford. I rang him at work. He was furious, but he agreed to meet me that evening. I could not stand the noise and dirt at my place any longer, so I spent most of the day feeling like an exile, sat in the Central Library on St Peter's Square, where it was warm and dry and quiet. And I read everything they had about Chile, which was not a lot, but better than nothing. By the time I met Clifford I was, in my own modest way, a bit of an expert. Tomorrow, I thought, I will learn everything there is to know about the copper industry. Maybe, I thought vaguely, I should start to learn Spanish. There are evening classes at the university.

We sat in Clifford's car in an unlit area beneath the motorway. Clifford had parked by a small basketball court. A bunch of kids were skateboarding in the darkness. If you listened carefully, above the roar of the traffic over our heads and the noise of colliding skate boards, you could just hear drunks singing and smashing glass on the main road. The silence between us had gone on so long I had begun to wish I was a smoker.

"This is a mugger's paradise," I said.

"Yup," said Clifford. "But they concentrate on students, and they mainly operate at the start of term, when the students have still got grant money in their pockets."

"We don't look like students."

"Not in this car we don't."

"So, what's going down Clifford? Anything new to report?"

"Why ask me? You called the meeting."

"Just showing an interest, Clifford."

"I can do without it."

"Do I sense a little hostility Clifford?"

"You might."

"So what's happening?"

"Nothing."

"Nothing?"

"Nothing. It's all gone quiet."

"So."

"So I think... honest... you've done enough. Now it would really be a whole lot better if you just, you know, turned it over, the whole thing, to the police... or at least let it drop for a while."

"Why, Clifford? Why is that?"

"Well... it might just... be safer."

"Safer. I see."

"Good."

"But we're on to something Clifford. I spoke with Solomon Da Silva yesterday."

"Yeah, I know. Just before he died. We heard some journalist was sneaking about at the hospital. I reckoned it would be you."

"Clifford. This is a big story... my big story. I'm not so old. I could coast into a new job with this one. Isn't that why you gave it to me? Isn't that what you wanted? And besides."

"What?"

"You are the police." Clifford punched the steering wheel. "Clifford, they haven't exactly stretched themselves on this one."

"You just don't understand. You should drop this whole thing. Right now. It's changed."

"Changed? How?"

"You just don't know what you're getting into."

"And you do?"

"I never said that. I had no idea. I thought it might be a good local interest story... a local bloke and all that. I didn't know where it was going."

"And now you do?"

"Not exactly."

"Clifford, your concern for my safety is touching, but it doesn't help."

"You are not listening to me."

"I'm listening. I'm listening."

"And?"

"Well, just think on this, Clifford. Agard did not die of a nasty cough. He was killed. Someone shot him, just a few days ago, in the chest with a shotgun. At close range, Clifford, at close range. Do you know what that means?"

"Means?"

"At that range a shotgun makes a hole big enough to lose a settee in."

"So what you're saying is?"

"So what I'm saying is: this is not a local interest story, Clifford. It never was. Whoever did this is not local. We are not dealing with local wide boys, and they are not playing at cops and robbers."

"You're talking bollocks."

"Maybe, but if you know something different."

"I should do what? Tell you?"

"Well tell me why you thought I had gone to Da Silva. Why me? Until I said I had seen him, you had no reason to link him to this case at all."

"Shit!"

Clifford thought about it for a moment. "I don't know anything for sure. Nothing more than you."

"Somehow, Clifford, I don't think that's true."

"And why's that?"

"I think you always knew a good bit more then you let on. I think you wanted to do me a favour, sure. But this has all got a bit serious, and you've lost control, and the big boys, whoever they are, are breathing down your neck."

"You don't know nothing for certain."

"I have the evidence of my nose Clifford."

"Your nose?"

"Clifford, you smell wrong."

"I smell?"

"No, you smell wrong."

"I'm black. To white people all black people smell weird."

"Unfair Clifford. Very, very unfair."

"If you say something like that."

"I never mentioned colour," I said. "Just listen."

"I'm listening, sister."

"And don't call me sister. What I'm saying is I remember how you smell, Clifford. I remember it very well. And I'm saying you now smell... wrong. You're scared."

"You should be scared too."

"Should I? Tell me."

"My wife... child... what would they do?"

"Come on Clifford. Do the right thing."

"Maybe I can't afford to at the moment."

"And what sort of a world do you want to bring your child into?"

"Leave it out!"

"Clifford, I read books."

"So what?"

"So in this one book these two old Jews in Warsaw are wondering if they should resist the Nazis. And the one says: 'I can't do it. I have a wife and child'. The other says: 'I must do it. I have a wife and child.'"

"Very clever."

"My point, Clifford, my screamingly obvious bloody point, is that you must tell me what you know."

"I... just... can't."

Clifford suddenly leaned over me, opened the passenger door, and gave me a hefty push. I was left kneeling on the wet pavement. He sped off out of the car park, past the wire netting of the basketball court. With screeching tyres and flaring brake lights he paused at the main road, then pulled out into the traffic and was gone.

It was the builder, Mr O'Malley, who let me in. He looked me up and down. My knees were bloody. I had mud all over me and leaves in my hair.

"Are you hurt at all?"

"No, I don't think so. Well, not much anyway. Just my pride. A little shaken."

"Boyfriend trouble, is it? Well now." He held my arm and helped me indoors. I went into the bathroom to dab some TCP on my grazed knees while Mr O'Malley braved the wreckage of my kitchen to make a pot of tea. I emerged from the bathroom, limping only slightly, just as Mr O'Malley placed a tray with tea and cups and a pint of milk on the sitting room table.

"That really is very kind of you. Were you just passing? Do you live around here? I didn't expect to see you today."

"Well now, if truth is told, I just popped in to check that the Acro-props were positioned OK. Sometimes kids come along and if they can get up the scaffolding, they like to play about with them. But that to one side now, you don't see me. And I'm not here if anyone should ask."

"I'm not sure I understand... who would ask?"

"Well, to be particular, if your landlord should contact you, in the near future, to ask awkward questions of my whereabouts at this precise moment, I'd be obliged if you didn't see me today and told him so."

"But why would he ask? And if he did, why would I say I hadn't seen you?"

"Well, let me pour you a cup of this fine brew and I'll tell you."

He poured cups of a brick coloured tea and splashed milk from the bottle creating swirling patterns. Then he sipped, sighed, and looked at the far corner of the room for a moment.

"OK Mr O'Malley, I'm ready."

"Well, if you are comfortable I'll begin, if it's all the same to you. I have to get back soon, or my wife will twig to what's going on."

122

"So, you'd better tell me, Mr O'Malley. The last thing I want just now is to have your wife getting hold of the wrong end of the stick."

"You wouldn't want her getting hold of the right end either."

"I think you had better explain."

"I didn't want to speak with the other fellers about, you know. And what I wanted to say was this. Your landlord is a friend of my wife, that's how come I do work for him sometimes. But for me he's just a first class shit. He told me you were a horrible person. He said I should do the work here, but I shouldn't never speak to you if I could avoid it. He said you'd have the law on me if I put half a word out of place. Have me in court and all that. But me and the boys have been here a few days, and... well... you've been OK with us. And we see the way you are. Anyway I feel a bit bad about things and what I wanted to say was this. When I'm not working for your landlord I buy up houses on my own account. I do them out and sell them on, you know?"

"I see," I said, but so far I didn't see at all.

"Well, the thing is your landlord is trying to sell this place and he's managed to buy off all the other tenants. Did you know that?"

"No... you mean he's actually paid them."

"Oh yes, the others are all paid to move out any day now. Have they not said anything?"

"Not a word. I don't have much to do with them. Hardly even see them."

"Well, I thought not. Anyway, he's a shabby bastard, if you'll pardon my lapse into the vernacular. But the thing is he can't sell this place while you're here as a sitting tenant. He can only get a fraction of the market price. So he's planning a few nasty surprises for you."

"What exactly?"

"Well, I can't really say. You know, he just comes on the phone to me from Singapore and says: 'Do this', 'Do that'. And I do it. I'm not party to his plans, but I know him of

123

old. I know he wants you out, and he wants to sell this place as soon as possible. He's got a new wife out there in Singapore, and he needs the money from this place to get rid of the old wife here, you know. Buy her off, make a divorce settlement. You're blocking him. I've worked for him before, you know, and you hear things. He's a very vindictive man… vindictive. Ask his wife… ex-wife."

"Mr O'Malley, it's very kind of you to tell me all this, but, I have a feeling that you are headed somewhere."

"Well, yes, indeed I am. Indeed. I want to buy this place from your landlord with you as sitting tenant."

"Why? What for? Are you mad?"

"Well, I hope I'm not any more mad than the next person. I want to buy it for profit, you see?"

"No, I don't quite see. I mean if I'm still here."

"Well, look… he's not offered you anything to move out, has he?"

"No. He's just told me to go."

"Right. Well, look. I think I can buy this place from him at a fraction of its market price, as long as you remain a sitting tenant. But then, when I've bought the place from him, I'll do you a deal. Right? I'll split the difference with you 50-50."

"The difference?"

"Yeah. The difference between what I pay for this place with you still in it, and the market value of the place without you."

"I see," I said, beginning to see.

"And, when I give you the money, you move out. Right?"

"Mr O'Malley… that's very good business. But what kind of money are we talking here?"

"Well, it seems to me, the market is skyrocketing at the moment. I have people ringing me up from London, paying good money for properties they haven't even seen. Whatever I pay you, I'll make it back within a short while. So, frankly, we're talking monopoly money."

"So it's a case of me helping you to buy the house cheap, then you offering me a large…"

"Largish."

"...sum of money."

"To help you on your way."

"I see."

"That's a fair summary of the plan, yes it is."

"And you don't have any guilty feelings about stiffing your boss."

"Just so long as my wife doesn't find out. This is business. As long as you're happy with me and our deal is straight."

"Aren't you afraid I might let you buy the place and then refuse to move?"

"Well, that's always a possibility, but I have a feeling you're in a bit of a rut, that you'd would quite like to move and…"

"Thank you Mr O'Malley, I think we can leave my motives out of this."

"Fine. I just sense that you want a change is all I'm saying."

"OK. fine. I want a change. Agreed. So run this past me one more time… just so I can begin to fill in a few of the details."

"So you're interested?"

"Very."

"Good. Good. So now you see why I'm not here?"

"The finer points of your invisibility are not wasted on me, Mr O'Malley."

"If either of them ever found out…"

"Not from me, Mr O'Malley. Now, details."

I went to bed that night feeling perhaps the future, if not bright, was slightly more pearly than it had been. If the deal with Mr O'Malley came off I could move out, get away, perhaps head off for London. I woke up smiling.

Almost as soon as I was out of bed Clough rang my doorbell. "I've just got off the Liverpool train. I've been very busy since I saw you last. You know, there's a few things we had running on the original investigation that I never had the chance to follow through. And this was one of them. Normally I'd have some young constable run this stuff down, but... anyway I needed the exercise. Christ this place is a mess. New cleaner?"

"I've got the builders in."

Clough lifted the sheet over the kitchen door and peered in. "Looks like they've tunnelled their way out. Didn't they realise they were on the first floor?"

"Come away from there and drop the sheet would you? I'm trying to keep some heat in the place."

We went into the sitting room, stepping carefully round the piles of crockery and pots. Clough took off his coat and draped it over a chair back, then opened up a large manila envelope. With a theatrical flourish he slapped two glossy black and white photographs on the table.

"Look!"

I looked. The first picture showed a man sitting in the shade of a tree in gentle sunlight. He held a book in his hand and looked is if he had been disturbed while reading, but he did not seem to mind. He was smiling.

"Who's that then?" said Clough.

"Dunno... I've only seen a couple of police file pictures, but it looks like Agard. Is it him?"

"Maybe.... OK, and who's this?" He pushed the second picture towards me. I picked it up. Agard, sitting sprawled across a stone bench. He looked relaxed and happy. He was wearing a denim jacket and jeans, and his hair was long.

"Agard... slightly different angle... a couple of years later... maybe?"

"Look again."

I took up the pictures and looked closely. Agard: floppy, blond hair, turned up nose. The other, just the same, even down to the creases on either side of the nose and from the corners of the mouth.

"OK. Two pictures. Different time. Different place. Same man."

"No. Two different men."

"Agard and someone who looks like him. Uncanny

126

resemblance... So what?"

"I have a contact who works in the passport office in Liverpool. He owed me a favour. Look at these."

He put two small black and white photographs on the table.

"These are passport photos," I said with some confidence.

"I know. So what d'you make of them?"

"I dunno... what? Agard had two passports? Different names? What?"

"No much simpler than that. These are two different men. One is Agard..."

"And the other?"

"Is Miller."

"Miller?"

Clough pulled out crumpled papers from his inside pocket and spread them over the pictures.

"Birth certificates. Agard and Miller were cousins."

"Bloody hell."

"My thought exactly."

I sat down to look at the papers.

"Well who'd have thought it? The resemblance is incredible... But hold on. There's more isn't there? I can tell there's more..."

"They were brought up together as kids."

"What happened to the parents?"

"Tragic. They used to go out together: dancing, a drink, you know. One night their car ran into the back of a lorry parked without lights. All four were killed instantly. After that their only living relative was an uncle in Galway. He was alcoholic and diabetic and couldn't take them in. He died shortly afterwards anyway. But he left them his smallholding — a cottage and a small plot of land."

"Is that where Agard hid out?"

"Most likely."

"So Miller and Agard kept in touch, even though they were sent to foster parents..."

"Possibly. More likely they rediscovered each other, as

young adults, through the legacy of the property in Galway. When they came of age the solicitors contacted them both..."

"But why did nobody know about this?"

"Because they never told anybody."

"A secret? Why?"

"Not a secret. Just private. Between them and nobody else."

"So all the time... nobody knew."

"But if I could find out this stuff, so could somebody else. I think they must have found him. Maybe he knew they were on to him. Maybe he ran to Dublin. Maybe they took him to Dublin... Anyway they caught him..."

"OK, but maybe that explains why Agard's computer disc was in the wall at Miller's house. But, why did nobody realise this before? Surely the police must have run a security check on Agard when they employed him?"

"I'm sure they did. But having a cousin isn't a crime: and being orphaned or fostered — they might be known and recorded somewhere, sure, but these are not security risks. They are not 'political'. And they don't come up on a crime sheet either. So, as far as the police and the Home Office were concerned Agard was absolutely clean."

"And he was clean."

"Absolutely. Clean as the proverbial."

"But people who saw Miller, the police who went to Druids Hill, the ones who saw Miller's body, surely they would have realised Miller looked like Agard?"

"No... I remember it very well. To be honest, you couldn't have said what Miller looked like after... I could hardly bear to look at the body."

"But the reports of Miller's death, the incident at the farm, Agard processed all this information..."

"And he said nothing."

"Not a word."

"Even to his own wife?"

"Apparently not."

"A real cool customer."

"Close mouthed. That's what his wife said about him... very controlled. In a way you have to admire him, the way he disappeared... even his wife didn't know where he'd gone."

"But why didn't he tell her something? Anything?"

"He was protecting her. Whatever he said would have put his wife at risk. She had to know absolutely nothing if she was to be safe... at least, if she was to live. If she had known anything at all, and these characters had got hold of her, they would have made her talk."

"So he was in Galway all that time. Did nobody think to check on that?"

"Nobody checked because nobody knew anything about it. He made sure of that. Nobody knew he had a cousin. And just when we might have started to uncover something, just when there was a good chance I might have found something, following up the leads, I was booted out and the case was allowed to drift until there was nothing left."

"Sorry. I wasn't criticising. Just..."

"Let's try to think positively here... There are still a number of questions that need to be addressed..."

"OK. Questions? Such as?"

"Well, we've made a family link between Miller and Agard, and that's good. But how close were they? Was there any political connection between them?"

"Not so far as I know. Miller had been a member of the Socialist Workers Party while he was at university, but drifted away from it. Agard was a member of the Liberal Party, then became a Social Democrat councillor for a couple of years, then seemed to lose interest. That's all I've been able to find out. But to be honest, I think they worked well together on a personal level, not necessarily anything to do with politics at all."

"No you're probably right. I was just wondering... you know with the CIA involved there could have been a political connection..."

"Such as?"

"Well, I was just wondering. I mean Miller collected statistics for the copper industry."

"I think that's politics enough, and that's the connection to the CIA, as far as I'm concerned. This has nothing to do with Moscow, if that's what you're driving at."

"You're probably right. But it was worth wondering... you did say we have to think about the context of the crime..."

"OK. Let's maybe keep an open mind on that. Who knows what we'll turn up next? But listen, what I want to know is this. Miller was killed *before* Agard went missing. Forensic said that Miller had brick dust and wallpaper paste under his fingernails *before* he died. That was several days *before* Agard replaced the hard disc. Whatever Miller was killed for, it wasn't Agard's copy of the hard disc, because that came later..."

"And because we can assume that as we discovered it, nobody knew about it until now."

"OK. Right. But if that's so, when did Agard manage to put his copy of the disc into the wall at Miller's house?"

"Good point. Hmm... I'd say Agard kept the disc in the boot of his car, waited until the police guard was taken off Miller's place, then sneaked back and hid it."

"But if Miller had brick dust and wallpaper paste under his fingernails before he died..."

"Before Agard hid the disc..."

"Go on..."

"Well... doesn't that mean that I found the disc Agard hid *after* Miller's murder."

"Quite so."

"And that means that even before Agard hid the disc, Miller had also hidden something..."

"And so?"

"And so, whatever Miller was doing to get dust and paste under his nails, that is what the killers were after. Something Miller had, not something Agard had."

"Good. And?"

"And whatever it was Miller hid, it's not the copy of the

disc. Miller didn't tell the killers where that was. It hadn't even been made when Miller was killed. The killers never found whatever it was Miller had hidden..."

"And that means...?"

"That whatever Miller hid, whatever he was killed for... Is still missing."

"That's right... Whatever this is all about, it's still to be found..."

"Exactly."

"Shit! That means it's probably still in the house. Which the builders are in the process of demolishing even as we speak..."

"No time to get the bus. Call a taxi."

I made the call, snatched up my haversack and we headed for Druids Hill.

Chronology: 16 October 1998-November 2000

General Pinochet was arrested in London while attending a clinic for back problems. Spanish Prosecutor Baltasar Garzon pressed for extradition of the General to Spain and presented evidence of 32 specimen charges against Pinochet. However, the British Law Lords reduced the charges against Pinochet. In response Spanish Prosecutor Garzon brought 43 new cases of torture and conspiracy to torture against Pinochet. Baroness Margaret Thatcher, on the other hand, expressed her support for General Pinochet, declared herself his ally, appealed for him to be sent home and visited him while he was under house arrest.

In July 1999 and again in November 2000 the US State Department, the Defense Intelligence Agency, the CIA and the FBI released 17,000 classified documents about US interference in Chile. This was the fourth batch of documents President Clinton had ordered released. The documents — all heavily censored — revealed that the US government had established support for opposition to Allende very early in his political career, financed opposition to his presidency and funded covert operations against his presidency. The documents established that the CIA had conducted a dirty tricks campaign against President Salvador Allende going back as far as the 1960s.

131

They had given $4,000,000 to the right wing opposition parties, spent $2,600,000 on the 1964 Christian Democrat election campaign, given $1,700,000 to the newspaper El Mercurio to criticise the Allende government, and had channelled $2,600,000 to US agents for covert operations in Chile. They had given logistical support to Pinochet's coup, maintained substantial links with the Pinochet regime, knew in detail about, and had connived at, human rights abuses under Pinochet. And the US government had gone on funding right wing organisations in Chile well into the 1980s.

Jaime Perez-Cervera & Maria-Dolores Jamon
Augusto: The Little Book of the General

It was starting to rain as we left the house. We sat in the taxi with the windows misted. Neither of us spoke. By the time we got to Druids Hill the rain had set in hard and steady. We approached the house cautiously on foot, weaving our way through the birch copse and then through the dense shrubbery on either side of the drive. They had made a start on the demolition, but were still stripping out the valuables and dealing with the outbuildings. They had not yet taken off the roof.

"Can you see anyone?" said Clough.

"No. And the lorry isn't here either. Look, the JCB is parked up and secured."

"Maybe they are off on another job."

"Maybe."

We made our way up to the house, knocked away the post that had been nailed diagonally in front of the jamb, and pushed open the front door. Even in the semi-darkness we could see that all the stained glass from above the front door had been taken out, the carved wooden banister, the fireplaces, the stained glasses round the door. They had also ripped out all the copper and lead piping from the walls.

"Builder's spoils," snarled Clough.

We started in the attic, where the rain was drumming on the roof, and went through the rooms, one after

132

another, looking for an out of place patch of wallpaper like the one I had found before. Clough shone my spotlight along the walls looking for telltale lumps and bumps, but we found nothing. Clough scratched his head and smiled. "Emma, this place is in better order than yours."

"I do my best."

"A basement."

"You want me to grovel? I'm so very, very, awfully sorry about the state of my flat. The builders, my cleaner, the cat."

"Idiot!"

"Abasement... you said."

"I meant a cellar. There has to be a cellar in a house this size. Somewhere to store cold meats, wine, pickles, vegetables for the winter."

After a short search we found a wooden panel let into the side of the staircase in the hallway. The panel creaked as I pushed it open to reveal wooden steps descending into darkness. I took the lamp from Clough and went down first, treading cautiously in the gloom. At the bottom there were three rooms, all in complete darkness. The first was just a box room, the second had lime-washed walls and an earth floor. I flashed the torch around the walls and discounted both. The third room was a kind of den. There was a stone-flagged floor, a mouldering sofa, a miniature pool table with curling baize, and in the corner there was a gold-lacquered drinks trolley with bottles and glasses. On the walls there were the tattered remains of sixties posters — Che Guavara, Jesus, Karl Marx with an eye patch. And opposite them was a dartboard riddled with holes. In the centre of the dart board the tightly bound card bulged through the steel frame, the bull's eye pushed out from the wall; around the edges the card hung through the wire frame in strips. It didn't look as if the demolition crew, or anybody else, had been down here. In fact it looked as if no-one had been down here since Miller's last visit.

"Hold the lamp," said Clough. He was staring at the dart board.

"What? You fancy a game?"

"I don't see any darts."

"No."

"And that board's seen better days."

"So it has," said Clough stepping closer and peering at it intently. "Heavy duty service, I'd say. Played almost to bits, right enough. But look, Emma. Don't you see?"

"See what?"

"The board is played to bits, but the wall around it has no holes at all."

"So?"

"So dart boards are usually surrounded by the marks of near misses — you know, when you're going for that last double-and-out."

"Sorry, I'm not a darts person."

"Well, let's just say that I have all the experience of a misspent youth to call upon. Even the best players miss once in a while... and everyone else misses constantly."

He eased the damp, crumbling dart board off the wall. It fell apart in his hands, the shreds trailing in strips and tatters down to the floor. "See here now. There's not a mark on this wall."

Clough took the hammer from my rucksack.

"Is this it, d'you think?"

"Dunno. Only one way to find out."

He began to swing the hammer against the bricks, showering me with dust, cement and debris. I skipped away to a safe distance. After a couple of minutes he paused for breath and took off his jacket.

"You'd have done better to pack a crowbar and a pickaxe instead of this wee toffee hammer."

"I'll remember next time."

He smiled grimly and went back to work. After about twenty minutes he had made a sizeable hole and removed six bricks. He put down the tools and shone the torch into the cavity, then he handed me the torch and leaned into the hole pushing his arm in up to the shoulder. He was on tiptoe, fishing with his fingers, grunting at something just out of reach. Then he smiled and relaxed, easing back from the hole. Carefully he pulled out a package and placed it on the floor.

"Bingo!" It was bulky bundle, a heavily waxed cloth wrapped over several layers of plastic sheeting and sealed with masking tape. Kneeling next to the remains of the dart board we unwrapped the tape and pulled off the sheeting. Inside there were bundles of documents — typescripts, photocopies and yards and yards of spooled paper tape.

Clough looked at the tape and grunted: "Telex."

"Let's take it back and read it where there's more light."

We stuffed everything back inside the plastic and then into my rucksack. Clough scuffed the remains of the dart board into a heap, as if it had just dropped of the wall. We surveyed the hole in the wall for a moment.

"Bloody great hole like that."

"Bit of a give away."

"Not much we can do about it though."

"Right, but anybody looking at it would know."

"Aye, that's what worries me."

"Well let's just hope nobody looks."

***

Harry did not seem surprised to see us. "I left a message at your place."

"I don't have an answer-phone Harry."

"No, it was your flatmate."

"I don't have a flatmate. I live alone."

"Oh. I thought it was... well... your domestic arrangement. Your live in lover, partner, boyfriend, the builders maybe. Whatever. Not my business. I just left a message."

I noticed Clough frowning.

"I think we may be running out of time."

"What do you mean?"

"I mean that you live alone, but Harry spoke with someone at the flat."

"There was someone in my flat?"

"That's what I keep saying," said Harry.

"Not the builders? Who? I mean..."

"Does it matter? You could take your pick: CIA, MI6, MI5, Chilean Intelligence, Special Branch, local plod."

"Yeah," said Harry. "They're all in on this somehow."

"That doesn't matter, the main thing is that we know that they know we know," said Clough.

"Yeah?"

"Is that the main thing?"

"Of course it is."

"And what do we know exactly?"

"A hell of a lot, actually. And more by the minute. So let's stay crisp."

"So, what have you got for me this time?"

"Lots and lots, Harry. The trick as always, will we be able to put it all together?"

Harry hauled a six pack of beer from under the settee and put it on the table.

"The thing is," said Harry. "If this is gonna be another all-nighter I'm gonna be comfy. There's glasses in the sink for them as needs luxury."

"I've seen the state of your china, china. I'll drink from the can."

I noticed Clough looking at me with a raised eyebrow.

"What?"

"Nothing. I was just remarking to myself that, for a women whose kitchen, on her own admission, is in a state of considerable disrepair you seem very willing to criticise Harry."

"True. You're right. I apologise Harry.

"Accepted," said Harry.

"That's more like it, said Clough. "Amity, concord..."

We sat around the table and pulled the papers and tapes from the bundle. The bundle from the wall of Miller's basement consisted of telexes, memoranda, case papers, press releases, planning documents, draft radio

136

and TV announcements — all years old, of course, dating from Miller's time at the Non-Ferrous Metals Service.

Everything was related to President Allende's death, but it was all dated to nearly two years before Pinochet's military coup. It was just as Da Silva had said. The CIA and Pinochet were prepared. They had laid their plans well in advance. It was a long, depressing read as we pushed each document round the table, from Clough to me, to Harry. At first almost every item caused us to whistle through our teeth, read extracts aloud, shake our heads in dismay. Then gradually we fell silent. Wearily, Clough ordered and piled the documents. It was another all-nighter, and it was early morning again before we surfaced from this other world of a decade ago. Weak daylight was showing through Harry's hideous lemon yellow and orange curtains. We were bleary, red-eyed, smelly, reeling with fatigue. Harry said:

"We should get these copied pronto. You know, this stuff doesn't just show General Pinochet to be a bit of a shit — we knew that all along — it absolutely shreds the CIA's claim they knew nothing about the coup until it happened. I can see the headlines now."

"Plausible deniability."

"That's the one. Shot to buggery."

"Just like Miller and Agard, in fact."

"Well if we can make this public."

"I'm not sure it will make any difference to anyone now," said Clough. "At the time maybe."

"Why do you say that?" said Harry.

"Just a personal feeling really. I wonder if you went out on the street and asked the average punter where Chile was on the map, they'd have a hard time."

"Yeah, well, I thought the Falklands was somewhere between Scotland and Norway."

"So you have Mrs Thatcher to thank for your improved knowledge of geography."

"I do. Just about the only thing I have to thank her for."

Harry wanted to get the documents copied at a print

shop as soon as possible. We climbed into his battered car, and he drove me and Clough, the slashed roof of the car flapping in the breeze.

"I know a good print works where we can get some bulk copying done."

"OK," said Clough, "but Harry I want you to drive real slow for the next few minutes. If someone is following us I want to make them absolutely bloody obvious to see, so crawl, Harry, crawl."

We crawled for the next fifteen minutes, but spotted nobody who looked like they might have been following. Eventually we turned back onto Wilmslow Rd, then Harry turned off down Oak Road, past the front of the Christie Hospital, driving real slow, as if he was looking for a place to park, which is a sick joke along there. Then he turned south onto Palatine Road.

Eventually he pulled over and parked outside Cohen's Printers. The owner was standing outside, taking a breath of fresh air, wiping his hands on his inky apron. He shook hands with Harry as if they were old mates. We said we had a load of copying to do. He laughed and tapped his finger to the side of his nose in a conspiratorial gesture. He ushered us inside and showed us a photocopier in the back room.

"We often stay up all night on a Thursday to make sure everything's cleared away for Friday night." I nodded as if I understood. He gave us an electronic key.

"You plug the electronic key in here, and then, as you make copies it adds up how many sheets you use. When you've finished you take the key out, give it to me and I know how much to charge you. OK?"

"Ain't technology grand," said Harry.

"What's the deal with the Friday?" I asked when the printer had gone.

"Jewish Orthodox," said Harry. "Finish work early on Friday night ready for the Sabbath."

"This could take a while," said Clough. "We need what? Four copies of everything?"

"What about the telexes? How will we copy them?"

138

"I don't want to cut them up and paste them onto paper. That would make checking their age and authenticity difficult."

"It would also take forever."

"OK. So let's copy everything except the telexes. We'll divide the pile into three — I'll do the first batch. Harry, you do the second. Is that OK?" We nodded agreement.

"Right, so, for the moment you two can go and find a cafe. Have breakfast if you like. Come and get me in about an hour."

Harry and I stood in the car park at the back of the print shop.

"It's getting very Jewish round here. Used to be very Jewish up around Cheetham Hill, you know. Garments. Tailor shops. Kosher cafes, everything. The whole place used to come to halt of a Saturday. All gone now though. Everybody moved out, up to Bury and beyond. Or down here, it seems. As fast as people made a little money they moved away. There used to be a Sephardic Synagogue up there too, you know? Jews from the Spanish tradition — the only one of its kind around here. Beautiful, it was. A ruin, now. There's talk of turning it into a little museum eventually, if they can get the money. But that takes time, and times being what they are."

"Harry, I'm beginning to realise there is more to you than meets the eye. However, at this very moment I want a cup of tea, not a history lesson."

Harry smiled and led me down a side street to Sonny Rappaport's tea bar. There were a couple of lorry drivers eating toast and drinking mugs of tea. Harry ordered steamed buns and lemon tea all round. I stirred my tea and watched Harry lick the icing from his bun.

"Harry, why are you doing this?"

"Well I've found that if you don't get the icing first it has a tendency to melt and run up your wrist."

"No. I mean *this*. I don't have you marked down as the idealistic type."

"Well, now you mention it. For a while I did think the

139

SDP were a bit radical... but, you know, you grow, you change."

"And this is all way beyond just wanting to get into my knickers."

"I live in hope."

"What about the Professor?"

"Mmm, yes... could be tricky. But you never know. Anyway there's no harm in flirting is there. Especially since you never take me seriously."

"Right, and now I know about the Professor."

"Ah, well now you mention her, she's actually part of the reason, I suppose."

"Curiouser and curiouser. How do you mean."

"She's second generation."

"Second generation what? Robot?"

"Nah.... in this country. Her family were from the border area between Poland and Czechoslovakia. They came here in 1938. Got out in time, before the war started. She has an older sister, Magda. Magda married a Chilean. Juan-Maria. Funny name for a bloke, Maria. Eh? Nice bloke, though. An actor. They never had kids, and I always thought that was bit strange. But me and him were having a bit of a drink one time... actually it was a real binge. They weren't getting on too well at the time, you know, so he was staying with me for a few days. And maybe he'd had a drop too much. Anyway, he told me a few things. In Chile, before the coup, he'd seen life under Allende change, how things were difficult, but how they all pulled together when things got rough. Bit of a socialist was our Juan-Maria. But then, after the coup, the Santiago police had come for him in the night. Arrested him because he was an actor who had worked, touring the villages and so on. And because he was in a trade union. They took him to a football stadium, he said. Kept him there for weeks, out in the open, sleeping on the concrete steps in the stands. Every so often they would come and take someone away for interrogation, and mostly they didn't come back. Then, he said, they were all taken into the dressing rooms and

140

the areas under the stands. The stands were emptied. And the reason was that they stood prisoners in the goal mouth, and machine-gunned them. They didn't want witnesses. Day after day, he said they could hear the machine guns. And he was sure they would not let him out alive after that.

When it was his turn to go for interrogation they stripped him and beat him. They put a wire round his testicles, beat his balls with a hose pipe. He sat there on my settee, pissed as a fart, and told me this. He said: 'They broke my balls, Harry. I mean it... that's why no kids.' They let him go though. They thought that would keep him quiet, you see. He was sure that one day they would come for him, to finish the job. And after he came to Britain he wrote about it for the newspapers. Didn't make any difference, of course. Eventually him and Magda agreed to adopt a child, but..."

"Where is he now?"

"He went back. He had a sister. Only surviving relative. 'Cos he couldn't have kids she was that bit extra special to him, I suppose. She disappeared when Juan-Maria was arrested. He didn't expect to hear from her, ever again. Then the International Red Cross contacted him. Said they had found her in a camp in the hills. The Chilean Consulate said it would be OK, guaranteed it, said, if he took her to England and neither of them ever came back it would be OK. So, he could go back to Chile and get her... but... we never heard from him again. She was bait. The kid was just bait. And it's those same bastards we're dealing with, isn't it?"

"Does that alter anything?"

"Nah. It's an incentive."

"Incentive?"

"Yeah. Makes it family business... sort of."

"You ever thought of marrying the Professor? I think she likes you."

"Really?"

"Yeah. Why not?"

"Well, you know, she was my teacher."

"So?"

"So nothing. Just that she always says I'm not the marrying kind."

"She's wrong Harry."

"Think so?"

"Know so. Ask her."

Clough was waiting on the door step of the print shop. He didn't seem pleased to see us.

"What kept you two then? I've just about done everything." He was clutching six bulging manila envelopes and a plastic carrier bag with all the original material lying at his feet.

"We said we'd do our share."

"You can only do your share if you're here to do it. You weren't."

"Ooh, snappy..." said Harry. "Well look, you give it to me and I'll sort out posting it off."

"No don't worry. I live just round the corner from a post office," I said.

"I wouldn't dream of it, Emma," said Clough. His irritation seemed to have suddenly disappeared. "I'll do it. Emma you look absolutely bushed. Harry, why don't we take Emma home now?"

"Yeah, OK. No problem. Just think of me as your private taxi service."

So we drove over to my place, the slashed roof on the car flapping all the way. We were frozen by the time we arrived. Clough asked Harry to stop at the corner. Harry pulled over and opened the door for me.

"I'll come in with you, Emma," Clough said. "Just in case. Harry, would you wait here a moment. If I'm not back in five minutes, if there's any trouble, get away as fast as you can, don't try to help."

"But."

"He's right, Harry," I said. "You have the documents here under the seat."

"OK!" Harry nodded, as if reluctant.

Clough and I walked up the street to my place. I could see the scaffolding and the plastic sheeting over the boards used to secure the hole in my kitchen wall. Even then I felt something else was out of place. But given that the builders had made such a mess of my place I could not have said what. I unlocked the front door of the house and went up to the first floor. The closer I got the more powerful the feeling became. Something was wrong. The lock felt funny as the key turned. I stepped into the hallway and turned on the light.

The place was a shambles. And it was not the kind of mess the builders made. The place had been trashed. Drawers had been emptied onto the floor, the wardrobe was tipped over, all my pictures and mirrors had been smashed. I found Maggie and Adolf on the floor in a puddle of water and broken glass. They were stiff and cold. There was no sign of Beastly — the wise little monster had probably legged it at the first sign of trouble. Clough found a chair amid the debris and placed it carefully for me to sit on. I noticed strange smells to the place. I could recognise cigarette smoke, brick dust, after-shave, sweat and.... something else. These were not smells I normally associated with me, my place or my things. Clough stood calmly in the middle of a sea of debris. He sighed as he appraised it wearily.

"The builder warned me... he said... my landlord might do something... to get me out," I said.

Clough shook his head.

"No lassie, no. This is a professional job. Your landlord could never afford these guys."

"What do you mean?"

And even as I asked, I heard a voice float up into my memory. Mrs Agard saying that her place had been robbed soon after her husband disappeared. That had been a professional job, the police had said so. And how did they know? Because the robbers had opened the chest of drawers starting at the bottom rather than the top, so that they could save time. I looked at my chest of drawers. All the drawers were open. They must have started at the bottom, I said to myself, and left each one open to save time. Clough noticed what I was looking at and nodded.

"Definitely professional."

The phone rang. It took me a while to find it. A voice said: "I think it's time we had a serious talk." The voice was smooth, the accent slightly clipped.

"Clifford? Is that you, Clifford?" I said, though I knew it wasn't.

"Druids Hill. Six o'clock."

"Where's my cat, you bastard? If you've hurt my cat."

The phone went dead. Clough put his arm around me. "You can't stay here."

Clough ushered me outside and waved to Harry. Harry pulled up next to us. Clough sat me in the car.

"The place is trashed," he said.

"So now we know that they know we know."

"Yeah. The only thing is they don't know exactly what we know."

"I'm not sure we know exactly what we know."

"But we still have the edge. They don't know what they are looking for. They're probably working on a strict need to know basis. Their boss hasn't told them very much."

"I think we should get right away from here," said Harry.

"Where to?"

"I think Emma should stay with you overnight Harry."

"No problem."

Clough asked us to drop him off at Oxford Road Station. In the sloping car park behind the Corner House Cinema he lifted the manila envelopes from under the seat, and pulled the plastic bag of photocopies towards him.

"I'll post the envelopes and take care of the copies."

It was not a subject I felt like discussing.

"I'd prefer to keep the originals with me," I said.

"Sure you would, but if they come looking..."

"If we split the stuff up there is a better chance they

144

won't get everything… if they come looking."

"Right," said Harry. "So let's split up the documents and the copies. You keep the copies, I'll take care of the originals, and Emma can hold onto the magtape and the discs."

Clough reluctantly released his hold on the originals. He set off for the ticket hall, clutching the envelopes. We watched him go. Harry said: "I just got a funny feeling. Emma, Clough's got… I'm just wondering. You know. Out loud… but he's got all the copies."

"Yes, but I've got the original disc, the magtape and the copied discs, and you've got the originals. What d'you think he's gonna do?"

"Dunno. Probably he'll just do like he said and post the stuff."

"Harry, you should be ashamed."

"Yeah… maybe you're right. It's just me being, well…"

"Suspicious?"

"Precisely."

"Even so Harry, I don't want the discs and tape at your place tonight. Just in case."

So Harry drove us round past the blue-green spike of the old Assurance building, down the narrow canyon streets, between the disused warehouses to the back of Piccadilly station. The left luggage office was sometimes closed because of the possibility of an IRA bomb, but we were lucky. Everything fitted snugly into a medium sized locker and it only cost us two quid for twenty-four hours.

Next morning I reckoned it was safe to go home. They [whoever they were] had already searched the place and found nothing. Why would they come back? And if they did, they would find nothing.

Harry drove me home, of course. It was still cold and messy and unfriendly. Brick dust had settled everywhere in a thick film. Everything felt gritty to the touch. Harry pushed aside the sheet over the kitchen door, filled the kettle with water and began to make tea, while I set about clambering through the neighbouring gardens to look for

Beastly. I called his name and rattled his cup. This caused a few curtains to twitch. But no sign of Beastly. When I got back to the flat Harry had made tea and found some biscuits. He'd even put them on a plate. He sat on the end of my bed. I sipped tea and began to sort out a few things from the floor. All my clothes — clean and dirty all mixed in together — were scattered across the floor. I was just about finished when there was a soft knock at my front door. Harry picked up a heavy table lamp and quietly took up position behind the door. He motioned with his eyes for me to answer the door.

Cautiously I peeped out into the hall. Mr O'Malley's bulky frame blocked the doorway.

"Have you forgotten? We have a meeting?"

"A meeting?"

"Ach! Don't say you're backing out. We have a deal! We agreed. I have my chequebook here."

"The deal! A cheque! My god, I'd forgotten all about it."

"How can you forget a thing like that?"

"I have a lot on my mind just now... come in, please."

He stepped into the hallway.

"Mr O'Malley, I'd like you to meet my friend, Harry."

"Pleased to meet you Harry. Mending the lamp, are you?"

Harry looked only slightly more guilty than usual, noticing the lamp in his hands as if for the first time."

"Yeah... I... I... just mended it."

"The bulb was it?"

"Yeah, the bulb, you know?"

"I do. I do," said Mr O'Malley, and looked pityingly at Harry.

"Oh, and before I forget." Mr O'Malley brushed past Harry, out into the hall, and returned a moment later with a large wire box. Beastly hissed a greeting from the depths of the cat carrier.

"Beastly! Where have you been?"

"He was behaving very strangely and you weren't around, so we decided to take him to the vet. I hope you

146

don't mind."

"Behaving strangely?"

"Yes, rolling around, making a terrible din. Sicking-up and frothing at the mouth. Anyway we caught hold of him in a bath towel and took him round the corner. And a good thing we did. The vet said he was poisoned."

"Poisoned? Somebody poisoned my cat?"

"Yes, well, maybe not. Cats scavenge, you know. They have no shame. Even if you feed them well, they still eat stuff off the streets, dead pigeons and the like."

"So what happened?"

"Ah, well now… they pumped his stomach. Washed it all out of him. The vet said we acted just in the nick of time. Another half hour and he'd have been a goner. Seems right enough now."

I slid the bolt out of the lock on the cage and lifted the lid. Beastly popped his head out still a little groggy. But Harry pushed the lid shut again and held it firmly, before Beastly had time to make his escape. Beastly wailed in anguish.

"Best if Beastly comes with us, I reckon," said Harry. "And I don't feel up to chasing him back into the box. Let him stay there until we get where we're going."

I noticed sticking plasters on Mr O'Malley's hands and fingers.

"Did he bite you, Mr O'Malley?"

"Well, I'm sure he didn't mean to."

"If he bit you, he meant to. He's not called Beastly for nothing."

"Well, that's not what we called him. But we couldn't let him suffer."

"That was so kind of you Mr O'Malley… was there a bill?"

He fetched a crumpled piece of paper from his pocket.

"Good God! A hundred and fifty quid! And you paid?"

"I'm sorry. We didn't know what else to do."

"That's quite all right, Mr O'Malley," said Harry. "Emma has Beastly back safe and sound. That's the important thing."

Mr O'Malley rummaged in his other pocket and handed

me a small phial of tablets.

"He's not quite right yet. He has to take these tablets morning and evening. I tried, but…"

"That's when he bit you. Mr O'Malley, I can't thank you enough."

"That's OK, but I have to get on shortly. Can we complete our business?"

"Business? Oh, of course, of course."

"Well, look I have the owner's agreement. He's going to sell me the place cheap. He reckons with you as sitting tenant he'll never get rid of it otherwise. So I'm going to make you an offer, right? And you're going to move out. Then I can do the whole place up and sell it on. At a modest profit, of course. And everyone wins on the deal. The owner gets to sell the house he neglected. You get paid to move out. I get a house to sell. So all we have to do now is agree a date by which you will leave."

"And when you will pay me the second instalment?"

"Right."

"A sum that will make us both happy."

"Right again."

"Mr O'Malley," said Harry, "correct me if I am wrong, but I would say you already have a buyer for this place. Am I right?"

"Right you are. I have a buyer, and the sooner we close this the happier I will be."

"Let's find somewhere to sit. You'll have to excuse the mess."

Mr O'Malley looked around, noticing the disorder for the first time.

"Looks to me like you should have words with your cleaner."

"It gets on top of me from time to time."

He shook his head sadly and did not look convinced.

"I think I'll make a fresh pot of tea," said Harry.

Mr O'Malley drank his tea without commenting further on my domestic habits and after half an hour of good-natured bartering I had a cheque for three thousand pounds clutched tightly in my mitt, with a second instalment promised for the day I moved out, and we had agreed a date.

Harry closed the door as Mr O'Malley departed. I waved the cheque at him. He took it, opened it up and read the figures. "Not a bad evening's work, Emma. Not bad at all."

"Right. And getting out of here won't be so hard now."

"And that leaves us with just the matter of getting your career restarted."

"Oh that again."

"'Fraid so."

Chronology: 1999

In August 1999 Amnesty International added its weight to those who believed General Pinochet should be put on trial. However, Baroness Margaret Thatcher condemned Jack Straw, the Labour Home Secretary, as 'vindictive' in his treatment of General Pinochet, attacked the Labour Government for its treatment of her 'friend' and praised Pinochet for bringing democracy to Chile. General Pinochet's supporters, ignoring his earlier statement that 'not a leaf moves in Chile that I do not know about', claimed he knew nothing of murder or torture, and that only communists would claim such things against him.

On 19 January 2000, Home Secretary Jack Straw reconsidered medical evidence that General Pinochet had suffered several severe strokes since his arrest and declared that he might now be medically and mentally unfit to stand trial. The Home Secretary declared that he was 'minded' to send the General back to Chile. Even before a final decision had been made public a Chilean Air Force plane landed at RAF Brize Norton to collect the General. However, such was the disbelief and international outcry against the idea that on 15 February 2000, Jack Straw was forced by the High Court to show medical reports on Pinochet to the Spanish, Swiss, French and Belgian authorities and to various Human Rights organisations.

However, after 18 months under house arrest in Britain, General Pinochet was finally set free by Home Secretary, Jack Straw. Under a heavy police escort the General was taken in secret to an RAF Air base where a Chilean Air Force plane awaited him. The General was presented with a gold plate taken from the Spanish Armada, a gift from Baroness Thatcher, inscribed with her name. As the plane took off the Home Secretary began his explanation of the release to the British Parliament.

Jaime Perez-Cervera & Maria-Dolores Jamon
Augusto: The Little Book of the General

Against all the advice from Clough and Harry, I wanted to go to Druids Hill. I wanted to meet the man who had trashed my place, killed my fish, poisoned my cat, the man who had put Clifford into such a spin. And I was definitely curious as to what he thought I had that he wanted so badly. Clough and Harry were absolutely against it, at first, but in the end they agreed. How else were we to find out what we were involved in, how else would we find out who was after the stuff, or even if we were on the right track. And what would they do to me? For all they knew I was the one person who knew where everything they wanted was.

"I'll just find out what is what and bring back a message. We can take it from there. Nothing else will happen, I'm sure."

There was something about the way Harry and Clough agreed, though. I knew they had not given up, that they would be up to something.

Harry did not offer me a lift so I went on the bus. I was only slightly surprised to see Clifford's car parked in the Druids Hill drive. I walked past it and on up to the front of the house. I noticed the contractor's vehicles. There was also a shed and a portaloo. I had not spotted these on the previous visit and surmised that the demolition crew must have brought them in since. I moved cautiously up the front steps and pushed open the front door of the house. A familiar smell lingered there, damp rot, dust, something else too, but I could not place it. From the hallway I called out: "Clifford! You there, Clifford?"

There was a long pause, then a voice came: "Down here. In the cellar."

"You coming up?"

"No. You come down."

"What? Down there?"

"I think you'd better."

I had a little warning bell in my head. I turned on the torch and made my way down the steps. Clifford was standing by the hole in the wall, with the rubble and the ruined dart board around his feet. A lamp sat on the floor. I switched off my torch.

"You know what this is?"

"It's a hole. I've seen one before."

"Very funny. Do you know anything about it?"

"They used to make vests out of them, didn't they, all tied together with string?"

"Do you know what was in here?"

"Why?"

"It's fresh. Somebody did this recently."

"Yeah, so?"

"So what do you know about it?"

"What's more to the point, what do you know about it?"

"Me?"

"You know something."

"Such as?"

"That this hole is recent. That something was in this hole. That this hole and whatever was in it are connected to Agard, connected to Miller... connected to me. Now, how do you know these things?"

Something moved in the darkness off to my left, and a figure emerged from the gloom. It was a man, a little old man, in his sixties at least, with grey hair greased down flat on his head. His shirt was too large for him around his scrawny neck. He was wearing short trousers and he was pointing a pump action shot gun in my direction. I raised my hands.

"I think we have had enough verbal fencing for one day." His accent was foreign. I expected Spanish, but he sounded German, and slightly American. And as he moved towards me his smell — the smell I had noticed when I

151

entered the building — wafted over me.

"Don't panic," he said.

"Why not?"

"Because it is already too late for that."

"Did you turn my flat into a rubbish dump last night?"

"No. And I would prefer to ask the questions."

"You've been here before, haven't you?"

"I have been to your very beautiful, very green, very cold, very wet country several times before. A long time ago."

"Were you wearing shorts then?"

"Shorts?"

"You must be freezing."

"Ah, my working clothes."

"The blow torch and the shot gun. That was you, wasn't it?"

"We did not manage to accomplish our professional objective on that occasion. I will not make the same mistake today."

"Very persistent for hired help."

"Hired? Who isn't? But I have my mission."

"Clifford, did you do a deal with these people?"

"We have an arrangement with Clifford," the old man said before Clifford could speak.

"I see. And is that how you got your promotion, Clifford?"

Clifford was silent.

"You silly sod... and just how long do you suppose this arrangement will last?"

"Don't mess with her," said Clifford, taking a step forward. Without even turning his head the old man swung the butt of the gun, hitting Clifford hard in the stomach, then he swung the barrel upwards catching Clifford in the face. Clifford dropped to the floor with a loud grunt. He rolled over, groaned and threw up onto the rubble. The man stepped back smartly to avoid getting his feet splashed.

"So, as I said, enough chit-chat. Don't worry about him. In a minute or so he will begin to breathe normally. But, little girl, he is right. I want prompt and full answers to my questions."

"Well I'm glad to see you still enjoy your work."

"I do." He pointed the shotgun towards Clifford, who was still retching on the floor. "I will ask a question. You will answer. If I do not like the answer I will shoot. I will not kill him, but he will wish I had. After two or three wrong answers he will have neither hands nor feet, and then I will progress along the limbs. When there is only a trunk left I will start on you, little girl. Are we clear?"

"Very clear, old man."

"Good."

"Where did you train for this line of work?"

"The Eastern Front. Belarus. I was just a boy, barely into my teens. A formative experience, believe me. That was when I realised I had a professional calling: anti-communist... and you know, since then I have never wanted for employment."

"Good God, how old are you?"

"Never mind that. I want to know. Now. What exactly was in the hole?"

"Don't you know what was hidden?"

"My instructions were not specific on this point."

"So you are like a mushroom — kept in the dark and fed on shit."

He raised the gun towards Clifford.

"I will not warn you again."

"OK! CIA documents."

"Documents regarding?"

"Proving CIA involvement in the coup led by General Pinochet."

"Good. And what was in the hole upstairs?"

I had to think quickly. Did he know about the magtape? Probably not. Did he know about Agard's hard disc. Maybe not, but he probably had some idea. And anything connected to Agard that looked as if it was important would be of interest. But there was no sense telling him about the magtape if he didn't already know. And if he felt he'd

153

wrung the disc out of me that might be enough to make him feel he'd got all there was to get. Either way it was a bit of a gamble.

"I'm waiting. I won't ask again."

"A computer hard disc stolen from the police by Agard."

"And on that disc? What?"

"Details of the police inquiry into the death of Miller, the man who held the CIA documents. Whoever had the disc could prove there had been some kind of intervention, a cover up, to prevent a police inquiry into Miller's death."

"A most precise account. I am so glad you have decided to co-operate. Now, where are these things?"

"In a safe place."

"So we must arrange to retrieve them at once."

"And then?"

"I let you both go."

"Unharmed?"

"Naturally."

"We're not idiots. If you get the materials, you'll kill us both."

"It is not for discussion."

"But then, if you don't get the materials, you'll kill us anyway."

"You will retrieve the materials!"

"Unfortunately, I cannot."

"Cannot?" He raised the gun towards Clifford, who was gasping and wheezing noisily. Even in the poor lamplight I could see his face was split, blood was running from his mouth onto his chest.

"The original materials — the disc and the documents — are in a safe place. But you see I copied the disc, the documents, everything. We sent them to the editors of *The Guardian*, *The Times*, *Financial Times*, *The Telegraph*, *The Economist*, *The Observer*... and several more besides. They are probably making their own copies right now, even as we speak. Tomorrow, or the day after, the whole story will be public knowledge. There'll be questions in Parliament, governments exchanging notes of protest, ambassadors recalled. I'd say the excrement has already hit the air filtration system."

"If that is so... then I must tidy up a few loose ends."

He raised the gun towards me, but as he did Clifford swung his foot at the lamp plunging the cellar into darkness. I flinched and dropped. There was a deafening bang. The shotgun blasted the wall where I had been standing. I was already moving, crouching, hands groping in front of me, towards the stairs. I could hear the sounds of a struggle but my fingers found the stairs and I kept on going. I heard another shotgun blast and the sound of plaster falling to the floor behind me. I stumbled into the moonlit hall. I could hear the old man cursing on the cellar stairs behind me. I ran down the hall, towards the front door, lost my footing on the storm step, stumbled through the door and out onto the gravelled path. I hit the ground with a thump that knocked the wind right out of me. In a second the old man was standing over me, wheezing, one hand twisted deep into my hair, the other pointing the shotgun at my face. He jammed the barrel of the gun into my mouth, banging it against my teeth. It was hot and tasted vile. I began to gag. He pulled the gun out of my mouth.

"It need not have been this way, little girl... but at least now I have your full attention."

There was a noise in the hall. Clifford must have followed us up from the cellar. The old man turned to see Clifford with a house brick raised high above his head lunging down the steps towards him. The old man fired as he turned. The blast threw Clifford back and sideways, his left leg a blur of blood and bone. He fell, screamed, clutched his thigh. Then, slowly he lay back and went quiet.

Breathing heavily the old man moved around Clifford and stood above him on the steps of the house. His bony knees looked blue in the pale light. He looked at me, looked down at Clifford and then slowly, very slowly he pointed the gun at Clifford's other leg.

"Let's put an end to this nonsense. Tell instantly, where

155

are the materials from the wall, or I will shoot his legs off — right here, now."

"OK. OK. Please. I'll tell you everything, only please don't hurt him."

I took a deep breath. I was just about to start telling everything I knew when the old man grunted. He appeared to dance several steps backwards. The gun fell from his hands clattering onto the steps. A fine mist of blood glimmered in the moonlight in front of his face. A feather had grown from his right shoulder. Still upright he was pinned to the stone pillar of the porch. He grunted again, but this time slower, longer. He clutched at the feather, twitching and groaning. His eyes rolled upwards, turned white, closed. His head fell forward and he went limp and he hung there.

I heard noises, running feet, voices. I could not have moved even if I wanted to. Harry the Hacker stood over me and Clough pulled me up into a sitting position.

"Come on, girl. No time to lie down on the job."

"I'm gonna throw up," I said and fulfilled my prediction spectacularly.

Clifford was lying unconscious. Blood was running down the steps in a stream. Clough stood up, opened his coat, took off his trouser belt, then knelt beside Clifford and in a very businesslike way began to make a tourniquet for Clifford's leg. While he worked Clough said over his shoulder:

"I have a new found respect for your hobby, Harry. It's definitely not a toy. Allow me to congratulate you on the accuracy of your shooting. Very fine, indeed. Is the bolt actually embedded in the stone?"

"Absolutely." Harry held up his crossbow, grinning in triumph. "You could hang off it if you wanted... well, actually, this geezer already is hanging off it."

"Amazing. I thought it would just bounce off stone."

"At this range? With a steel-tipped bolt? You could pierce armour, chain mail...."

"Very impressive."

156

"Easy-peasy, mate. You should see me with a bag of apples!"

"Watch out William Tell, eh?"

"What about the Boy Scout here. Should I get him down?" said Harry.

"No, let the bastard stay there until we get an ambulance."

"That could be a good few minutes."

"You're right," said Clough smiling in the dim light. "It could be a few minutes." Neither Clough nor Harry made any attempt to release the old man.

Harry put the crossbow down and helped me to my feet.

"How's Clifford?" I said. "Is he all right?"

"He'll live," said Clough trying not to look at the bleeding pulp of Clifford's leg. "He's out of it for the moment. He wasn't a keen dancer, I hope."

"Not that I'm aware of."

Clough picked up the shotgun from where it had fallen. He sniffed the barrel, squinted at it sideways, then pointed it at me in a businesslike fashion and said quietly: "Now don't get excited, either of you."

Both Harry and I raised our hands as if we were in some cowboy movie.

"What's all this about then?" I said, trying not to be surprised.

"I think you know very well what this is."

"So."

"So, I'm about to take my leave of you. With the evidence, of course."

"Shit."

"Not all the evidence?"

"Not all, true. But enough, I think."

"So what have you got?" said Harry.

"The photocopies."

"What about the other stuff?"

"I tried. The Boy Scout didn't do your flat, Emma. It was me."

"You have friends in low places."

157

"I do. A little legacy from my line of work, you might say."

"And my car?" said Harry.

"No. That wasn't me. It was probably the Boy Scout. But he didn't know what he was looking for. Even now, I reckon, they don't know exactly what you've got. They just know you've got something."

"The magtape, the original discs, the compact disc copies?"

"Yes it would have been nice to have them, but I reckon that if I couldn't get them by stealth, the only way I can get them now is by hurting you... and I don't want to do that."

"But the documents from the wall... look, there's no point."

"We have the originals and we copied everything," said Harry.

"Is that a fact? Or should I say was that a fact? Harry I had your place watched. By now I have the originals — all of them."

"Friends in low places again."

"Precisely. And, you've guessed, of course that I didn't post off any of that stuff to the newspapers."

"No," said Harry. "But guess what? I did."

"Yeah," I said. "We sent copies out to the newspapers. Harry guessed what you were up to. So he kept something back."

"Don't bullshit me."

"Harry arranged it all. What your mates have nicked from Harry's is just another photocopy. The original is safely locked away."

"You're bluffing."

"Clough, why would we bluff?"

Clough sighed and looked around him, clearly wondering what to do next.

"Clough why are you doing this? I thought you were a good guy."

"What a question. Well, let me see. I'm sick of the climate.

I'm tired of living on a scabby pension. I'm tired of minding pennies. I'm tired of... d'you realise the high point of my day for the last ten years has been going for a run over the golf course. What kind of life is that for someone like me? I'd have been perfectly happy working out my days, putting in the time to an honest retirement. But I was given the boot long before my time. I was cut off. I have intelligence, expertise, knowledge, skills. Somebody of my calibre... denied gainful employment... I'm still an active person. I've got an inquiring mind. And I've had to endure. Like some stone in the mud. I've had to wait my moment."

"You should have got a hobby mate," said Harry.

"Well, I saw a chance to put things right," said Clough, ignoring Harry.

"Right? How is this putting things right?"

"Ah... my right... different from your right. I'm talking about my right. You are talking about... well, who knows? Something obscure, abstract, moral. Yes?" I could not think of anything to say. Even Harry had fallen silent.

"The world doesn't work that way, Emma," Clough went on. "You can do the right thing. You can spend your whole life doing the right thing. And you can still get shafted. I mean, even young Clifford here is on the take, eh?"

"You're gonna get shafted if you go through with this, mate. That's for sure," said Harry finally.

"I'll make a deal. They can have everything, yeah? In return for a very large lump sum paid into a Swiss bank account."

Harry spat on the floor. "Never did like the Swiss."

"Somebody must pay. Compensate me."

"Who? The police? The CIA? Pinochet's lot? The Town Council? The Women's Guild?"

"Yes. Any one of those will do. I would prefer the bastards that caused the problem in the first place, but frankly I really don't care who."

"Clough you don't have much to bargain with. No discs, no original documents, no magtape, just a load of photo-

159

copies. So what have you got really?"

"Enough to alert them."

"Clough, they will kill you."

"We know you got screwed," I said. "But this won't help."

"Ah, well, you see, it won't help you, that is true. But then, I'm aiming to help myself."

"Maybe we can do a deal"

"Who with?"

"Well..." the more I thought about it, the dafter it seemed. "The police," I said lamely.

"The police. Yeah," said Clough, smiling. "A deal. Sure."

The German twitched and moved his head, as if regaining consciousness.

"Emma," said Harry quietly. "I think we should concentrate on getting these two to a hospital, before they bleed to death."

"Yes," said Clough. "The old chap looks like he needs a check-up, and Clifford is looking decidedly peaky. Just one last thing before I go. If I were you, I'd get rid of the tape and the discs. You see, although I failed to get hold of them, my deal will be to tell the Chileans or the CIA or whoever it is, just where those things are, who has them. Then they will come looking for you and if you don't give them what they want they will kill you. There's plenty more Boy Scouts just like him." Clough gestured at the German pinned to the pillar.

"It's more likely they will just kill you," I said. "And then us."

"Not necessarily, Emma. Not if I box clever."

"Good of you to warn us, Clough. Very decent, I'm sure."

"And what about you Harry? Anything profound to say at this fond moment of parting?"

"My arms are getting tired so kindly fuck off. And yeah, yeah, we know, don't follow or you'll shoot."

"Ah, you've read the manual, seen the film, excellent. Nobody move for at least five minutes. I don't want to hurt you — I even like you both — but I will if I have to."

160

And with that he turned and ran into the darkness towards the standing stones.

"Shit, shit and double bloody shit," said Harry between his teeth. "I just knew somebody as badly dressed as that..." He made a move towards the crossbow.

"No Harry. He'll kill you. He means it. A crossbow against a shotgun would be suicide." Reluctantly Harry agreed.

Chronology: March-November 2000

Upon his arrival in Chile General Pinochet, who in Britain had been unable to walk and confined to a wheelchair as a result of brain damage caused by a series of strokes, was seen to rise from his wheelchair and walk unaided. Unable in Britain to recognise anyone as a result of brain damage, upon arriving in Chile Pinochet was seen to recognise and greet members of his family and representatives of the military he had last seen some 18 months previous. British newspapers dubbed him 'General Pinocheat'.

On 29 January 2001 the Chilean authorities placed Pinochet under arrest and charged him with responsibility for more than 70 murders committed during his leadership. However, in July 2001 the Chilean Supreme Court suspended proceedings saying Pinochet was no longer mentally capable of understanding a trial.

Jaime Perez-Cervera & Maria-Dolores Jamon
Augusto: The Little Book of the General

Back to the present...

"And that, I finished rather lamely, that was the man I saw in the alley. The little German. The one Harry shot with his crossbow."

"Are you sure?"

"As sure as I can be after all this time."

"But he must be absolutely ancient by now."

"Ancient, yes. But clearly still active in the cause."

"Whatever that might be."

My husband sat quietly for a while. The windows of the car had steamed up. I could hear the wail of an ambulance siren in the distance. The policewoman had long since given up on the mouth to mouth, and draped the man with her coat. It glistened in the rain.

"I think he's had it," my husband said. "Poor bugger."

"I wonder if he has family here."

"Did any of this ever come out? I mean, I don't remember reading anything about it. Was there even a trial?"

"Well if there was I missed it. Clifford retired. Had to. Lost his leg below the knee. His wife didn't like that. I think she realised he'd been up to dodgy stuff — and I don't suppose doing deals to get a promotion was the end of it with Cliffie. Anyway she waited until a couple of weeks after the kid was born and Clifford was able to get about a bit on his new peg leg and then she left him. He wasn't half upset about it. Still, he got a police pension. It was all very convenient. With Clifford forced to retire injured, the police didn't have to sack him. After his wife left him Cliffie went to live with relatives in Jamaica. Clough — well, nobody ever heard from him again. Disappeared without trace along with most of the evidence. I fully expected to hear about his funeral once the Chileans caught up with him, but I dunno... maybe he pulled it off after all. Maybe he really did do a deal and retired on the proceeds."

"Harry the Hacker is still around, of course. Very respectable. Local luminary. Member of the Rotary Club. Probably a Mason too, by now. Owns a chain of shops."

"Computers?"

"Of course. Strictly legit. Nearly."

"What about Mrs Agard?"

"Miller's property went to Agard. And then Agard's property went to his wife. It took a long time to sort out, but in the end she was very well provided for. Went into a posh little nursing home I understand. Cut her daughters out of her will completely, left everything to the nursing home and the district nurse."

"And the Non-Ferrous Metals Information Service?"

"Business as usual. Went right on doing what it had always done."

"And the German, or whatever he was, the assassin?"

"Never charged. He had a Chilean diplomatic passport. They expelled him. A little thank you to Chile for services unspecified. We owed them, apparently."

"The SAS used Chile during the Falklands war, to infiltrate Argentina." There was a long silence.

"Probably that, then. Or something like."

"And Mr O'Malley?"

"Sold the house over the telephone to a Yuppie from London who had not even clapped eyes on it. Made an enormous profit just before the bottom dropped out of the property market. Two weeks later and he would have been forced to hang onto it for the next ten years at negative equity. And with the proceeds Mr O'Malley left his wife and went to live in Majorca."

"What about Beastly?"

"Beastly died quietly, sitting in my lap."

"Poison?"

"Old age. He was fourteen."

"Bloody hell. In cat years that's…"

"About the same age as General Pinochet."

The ambulance arrived finally, its two-tone siren blaring, its blue light flashing. A paramedic jumped out and knelt by the man on the floor. He brought out a stetho-scope and listened a moment. He shook his head and stood up slowly. A senior police officer strode over to the ambulance driver: "What the fuck took you so long?"

"Computer's down. But I could ask you the same question. Where the fuck were you when this happened?"

"Watch you fucking lip, pal."

The policeman turned and walked away. My husband said "Poor bastard. And what about your story?"

"The editors knew what had happened. They had copies of all the material."

"Hold on. I thought Clough didn't send the stuff out."

"Aha! That's right. But you see, Clough and Harry and I weren't together all the time that last day. What I didn't realise was that Harry was a little jealous of Clough. He didn't trust Clough at all. He noticed that when I asked Clough to make four copies of everything, he made six. So when Clough and I went into my flat to find it had been trashed, Harry took the opportunity to open one of the envelopes and take out the contents, the copies. In its place he put a couple of computer magazines. Clough never noticed. And then later, before following me out to Druids Hill with Clough, Harry popped round the corner to the local Prontoprint and had them copy everything. And that, along with the disc copies I had him make, was what he sent out."

"So you weren't bluffing after all."

"That's right."

"So, really all Clough could do was show the stuff to the Chileans or the Americans or whoever they were, and say this is what *won't* be appearing in the newspapers."

"That's it."

"Not much of a coup."

"Not very impressive at all."

"You devious bugger."

"Well, Harry's the really devious one. I hadn't got a clue, but he had Clough clocked from the start."

"So, as a result of Harry's efforts, you had offers of work

164

from all the big names in Fleet Street."

"Exactly. And of course I'd already had an offer to get out of the flat, and the money to do it."

"So you could move away, finally, and live on Easy Street."

"Well not exactly Easy Street. I still had to earn a living."

"Is that when we met?"

"Yes, not long afterwards. An off-day in the news room. I had to interview a local sporting personality — a real tasty geezer — this cyclist with a shelf full of medals."

"I remember. So what happened? Did nothing come out at all?"

"The government slapped a D-notice on the whole thing, so the papers couldn't say a word. We appealed, even went to court, but we lost. Couldn't even report the court hearing. Not a thing we could do. And we were warned never to speak of it in public."

"Or?"

"Or we'd face prosecution, of course."

"Did he recognise you, the poison dwarf?"

"He made a gesture." I showed the gesture, my hand shaped like a gun.

"Shit. On the other hand, who knows who he is working for now? It could be they recruited your poison dwarf, rather than prosecute him. He could be working for us now."

"And who would 'us' be?"

"Hmm... scary. I see why you were so rattled. I had no idea."

"No. It's not the kind of thing you chat about, is it?"

"Definitely not."

A policeman tapped on the car window. My husband wound it down. "We'll need to take a statement from you, sir."

"Of course... a statement. And will that do the trick, d'you think?"

"I beg your pardon, sir? Trick?"

"You know, bring him back to life?"

The policeman raised his eyebrows.

"You are the Greater Manchester Police. Your boss talks to God. And you haven't cracked how to bring people back from the dead?"

"No, sir. We haven't quite sorted that one yet."

The policeman saluted and backed away. I said: "What should I tell them? Should I tell them about the man in the alley?"

"I think so. I think you should tell them everything."

"Do think it will make a difference?"

"No, it won't make any difference at all, but tell them anyway."

"I'm not sure a fresh-faced young copper will understand."

"No, maybe not. But you will be a kind of walking history lesson."

Chronology: 2004-06

In the summer of 2004 the Chilean parliament awarded financial compensation to 35,000 of the surviving victims of torture from the Pinochet regime. At the same time Pinochet's bank accounts were seized as part of an investigation into the source of his estimated £6.3 million holdings and several senior officers were arrested for crimes committed under Pinochet. In December 2004 the Chilean Parliament voted to strip Pinochet of his self-awarded immunity from prosecution and he was accused of playing a major role in planning a 1974 car bomb attack against a Chilean Army General who had opposed the coup.

At about the same time Pinochet gave a lively and articulate interview to Maria Elvira Salazar on Miami TV in which he said: 'I harbour no hatred or rancour. I am good. I feel like an angel'. After this performance the Chilean Supreme Court reversed its previous ruling that Pinochet was too damaged by strokes to stand trial: it decreed that 89 year old Pinochet should be placed under house arrest and charged with a group of nine specimen cases of kidnap and murder relating to the 1973 Operation Condor – an intelligence sharing operation between five South American dictatorships designed to identify and 'disappear' hundreds of left wing activists and opponents. Included among the victims in the specimen charges was a group of Pinochet's opponents extradited from Argentina at Chilean request and never seen again.

In October 2006 investigators accused Pinochet of shuffling a total of $28,000,000 in and out of 128 US bank accounts in a complicated money laundering operation. A variety of other accounts around the world were later revealed. A further $160,000,000 of gold [approx 9 tons or three cubic meters] had been found in Pinochet's undeclared HSBC bank account. At about the same time Pinochet was charged with a further 36 cases of kidnap, one of murder and 23 cases of torture.

At Pinochet's death on 10 December 2006, Michelle Bachelet, the Chilean President and one of Pinochet's torture victims, announced that the government would neither honour Pinochet with a period of official morning nor give him a state funeral. Later that night riot police in Santiago dispersed angry supporters of Pinochet who had clashed with crowds celebrating his death with street bonfires and champagne. Clashes between the two groups continued until after the funeral. Plans to bury Pinochet in the family vault were abandoned for fear of desecration. Pinochet was cremated and his ashes returned to his family. At the funeral Pinochet's son said: 'He gave everything for his country. He pulled it out of tremendous chaos.'

The novelist Isabel Allende, niece of President Allende commented: 'I would have preferred for the courts to have finished their work. I wish there could have been a conviction and a sentence.'

Jaime Perez-Cervera & Maria-Dolores Jamon
Augusto: The Little Book of the General

Acknowledgements

I would like to thank the Writers' and Translators' Centre of Rhodes. My thanks also go to Steph & Mike Peters, Philip Painter and Ian Tighe (heroes from the age of steam-powered computers), Tommy 'Trumpet', the Chilean exile community in Swansea, Mary Niesluchowska, Brigid Benson, Joannie Joffe and — as ever — Madeleine & Luke Rose.